CROSS OF GOLD

CROSS OF GOLD

TIM CHAMPLIN

FIVE STAR
A part of Gale, Cengage Learning

GALE
CENGAGE Learning®

Detroit • New York • San Francisco • New Haven, Conn • Waterville, Maine • London

LIBRARY OF CONGRESS CATALOGING-IN-PUBLICATION DATA

Champlin, Tim, 1937–
  CROSS OF GOLD / Tim Champlin. — First Edition.
    pages cm
  ISBN-13: 978-1-4328-2790-8 (hardcover)
  ISBN-10: 1-4328-2790-1 (hardcover)
    1. Gold—Fiction. 2. Gold theft—Nevada—Lodestar—Fiction.
  3. Nevada—Fiction. 4. San Francisco Bay Area (Calif.)—Fiction. I.
  Title.
  PS3553.H265C76 2013
  813'.54—dc23   2013019122

First Edition. First Printing: October 2013
Find us on Facebook– https://www.facebook.com/FiveStarCengage
Visit our website– http://www.gale.cengage.com/fivestar/
Contact Five Star™ Publishing at FiveStar@cengage.com

Printed in Mexico
1 2 3 4 5 6 7 17 16 15 14 13

CROSS OF GOLD

CHAPTER 1

"Where's my gold?" Ezra Pitney, owner of the *Tiger Eye* and *Overstrike* mines, drove the question home like a railroad spike.

"Lodestar."

"Lodestar?" Pitney's pointed, gray eyebrows raked up and away from his black eyes like the spiked horns on a sidewinder. "What the devil is a lodestar?"

"A ghost town two days' ride east of here." Marchal Charvein slapped his hat against his thigh and dust flew into the shafts of sunlight lancing through the front window. He wished he'd taken time to clean up and have a good meal and a night's sleep before coming to this Virginia City mansion to collect his pay.

"Where's that bastard who stole it—Denson Boyd?"

"Dead."

"And his two partners?"

Charvein shrugged. "You might know better than I. They were headed for Virginia City last I heard—being trailed by a posse."

"I suppose you'll give me and the sheriff a full explanation."

"When I get rested up in a day or so."

"So you didn't bring the gold back with you?"

"Didn't have a spare pack animal. I was nursing a wounded woman, and we were both about done in."

"Did you recover all of it?"

The cold-blooded reptile has no curiosity about the woman or her injury.

"No. I don't know how many ingots were taken from that train five years ago, but roughly a hundred pounds of bullions left."

"Where's the rest?"

"A solitary desert rat found it not long after it was hidden in a cave by the robbers. He spent a little for supplies to stay alive during the past four years or so. Part of it he melted down and fashioned into two bell clappers. He didn't have the skill to cast a bell for the old church, so he made the rest of the gold into a cross and stashed it under the altar."

"Huh! A religious thief. Is he still there, guarding my gold?"

"Naw. He disappeared into the desert while I had my hands full with the woman and a couple o' gunmen." *Close enough to the truth for Pitney.*

The lean millionaire shrugged out of his gray suitcoat and flung it over the back of an armchair. His black, pomaded hair glistened in the afternoon heat. Charvein noticed his center part was crooked. "So all I have to do is round up a stout man from one of my mines, take some grub, water and a wagon, drive out there and gather it up."

"Better add a couple picks and shovels to that load," Charvein ran a calloused hand over the grubby beard he'd grown since he'd left three weeks earlier to track Denson Boyd into the desert. "The gunmen set Lodestar afire and half the town burned down, including the church. The gold's buried under a big pile of rubble." He neglected to mention he and the "desert rat," Carlos Sandoval, had dynamited the church to trap Denson Boyd and renegade lawman, Buck Rankin, inside.

Pitney snorted. "Anything else you might have forgotten to tell me?"

"Nope."

Pitney went to his suit coat and retrieved a small leather drawstring poke from the side pocket. He opened it and poured out a handful of $20 gold pieces, counted out a dozen and put the sack away.

"There you are—$240—payment in full, as agreed." He caressed the twelve double eagles in his slender hands, as if reluctant to let them go. He arranged the gold coins in two neat stacks on the marble-top table by the picture window where the afternoon sun could flood them with glowing light.

An old gambler's trick to make the amount look bigger, Charvein thought, scooping the coins into one hand and dumping them into a side pocket like so many pennies. "As agreed," he echoed. "And I earned every dollar of it, ten times over."

"Come, now," Pitney's nostrils flared as he raised himself to his full six-foot height. He hadn't invited Charvein to sit down while they conducted their business. "That's a sizeable amount of money. It represents nearly two months' wages for one of our overpaid union miners."

"Miners don't get shot at. If I'd known what I was in for, I would never have taken the job," Charvein stated bluntly.

"But here you are, back again, hale and hearty." Pitney favored him with an oily smile from beneath the pencil-thin mustache. The smile didn't change the rest of his face. The gray eyebrows continued to rake up at an angle above the black eyes.

Charvein took a deep breath and looked away. *Take the money and get away from here,* he thought. *This man has done you no harm. He's only paying you for a job performed.*

The lean man toyed with the burnished garnet on his watch fob. "We all take gambles in life, Charvein," he dropped any pretense at being affable. "I never hesitated to gamble. That daring, plus a lot of hard work, has paid off handsomely in my case." He casually gestured at the elegant living room of his hilltop mansion.

Sheer luck, Charvein thought. *If Providence hadn't smiled on you, you'd still be washing glasses in a Virginia City saloon.* He

9

nodded and turned to leave.

"Oh, just one more thing." Pitney slid a folded slip of paper from his vest pocket. "Sign this receipt and we'll be square."

Charvein followed him to a side table where he flipped up the cap on an inkwell, dipped the steel nib and scrawled his signature across the bottom of the receipt Pitney had already made out.

Pitney blotted it and folded it back into his pocket.

They didn't shake hands or speak. Charvein let himself out the front door, closing it quietly behind him. He took a deep breath of the hot wind. It was good to have that done with. He regretted only that he hadn't held out for more money when Pitney first approached him about the job of trailing released-prisoner Boyd to the stolen gold. Unemployed and broke, Charvein had jumped at the first offer—$240. No matter. He'd know better next time.

On the way back from Lodestar, he and Lucinda Barkley had parted company at her parents' home in Carson City, a few miles to the south. They'd care for her leg wound and listen to her story of abduction and danger. Maybe this experience would bring her down to earth. She'd been so caught up in medieval romance—with its knights errant, royal courts, wandering minstrels and the like—that she could hardly focus on the real danger that surrounded them. Yet, she did have the presence of mind at the end to shoot a dying Buck Rankin when he was about to put a knife into the sleeping Marc Charvein. For that, he would be forever grateful.

He now enjoyed a little financial breathing room, he thought as he mounted his mule and started down the hill toward the center of Virginia City. But this was still a boomtown, and these double eagles wouldn't last long, considering the prices of everything. Money flowed like the Carson River here. Everyone—from bartenders and prostitutes to businessmen and gamblers—bought and sold mining stock. This stock represented millions—if one could actually locate and extricate the rich veins of silver and gold from under hundreds of feet of rock ledges. The trick was in knowing, or guessing, which of the ornately printed stock certificates represented real wealth. The majority of the gilt certificates—to paraphrase Shakespeare—were full of sound and fury, signifying nothing.

Virginia City, with its hell-bent attitude and amorphous, get-rich-quick population, had been his home for the past few years, and he'd gotten used to it.

He dismounted at a barbershop for a much-needed haircut and shave, instructing the barber to whisk off even the mustache. The barber, in a hurry with three customers waiting, was not inclined to talk. This was fine with Marc, who was so tired he dozed under the steamy towel.

Later, he stepped down, freshly scented and smooth-faced, and tipped the barber an extra quarter for a job well done.

Next stop was the mercantile where he bought a new pair of canvas pants, a cotton shirt, a set of underwear and socks. From there it was only a short walk to Ki-Ling's bathhouse where he reveled in a good twenty-minute soak in hot, soapy water. He emerged from the wooden tub free of the trail grime, if not the memory, of the roaring, suffocating dust storm on the playa near Lodestar.

Emerging from the bath, he changed into his new clothes. The ones he'd been wearing for three weeks were full of tears, burn holes and ground-in dirt, and he dumped them into a trash barrel in an alley—but kept his Stetson, his vest and his short boots.

Marc's mount—one of the late Denson Boyd's mules—was as tired and dirty as he was so he turned the animal into a livery for a good feed of grain and a wash.

He handed the liveryman a three-dollar gold piece. "Give

him a stall with plenty of hay. He needs rest. I'll call for him in a day or so."

He would never think of Lodestar again without seeing and smelling the thick dust that never seemed to lie quiet. That dust, along with the dark, Indian features of Carlos Sandoval who'd saved his life, would be two things that would stick in his memory forever. Where would Sandoval go? What would happen to him? It would be good to know the small man's fate, but it was also unlikely they'd ever meet again.

Virginia City was nearly as wild, day-to-day, as his shootout in Lodestar. But, unlike the men who'd invaded the ghost town in the desert, no one here was gunning for him. Any shots he heard came from the dozens of saloons up and down the streets—celebrations, arguments or even suicides. The raucous revelry along C Street usually began after sundown, when the shifts changed at the mines. He smiled to himself that there was even something comforting in the familiarity of Virginia City and the adjacent town of Gold Hill—the grinding ore wagons, the shrill steam whistles of trains, the braying of mules, the tinkling of music from hurdy-gurdys in the open saloons, the distant thumping of stamp mills crushing ore day and night and the shouts, laughter, breaking glass, occasional shots. It all blended into a constant growl, like the low rumble of surf he'd heard as a child on the California coast.

As he stepped into a restaurant for his only meal of the day, he glanced up at a passing carriage—and stopped dead. The face of Lucinda Barkley was turned toward the driver—a local small-time gambler named Samuel Stonehouse. Her familiar laughter floated back to Marc as the open buggy rolled past, drawn by a trotting black Morgan.

He was stunned. Hadn't he just left Lucy off at her parents' home in Carson City early this morning? What was she doing in Virginia City? She must have bathed, changed into a clean dress and caught the next train north. He shook his head. Maybe he was mistaken; the girl in the buggy must've been someone who resembled Lucy. That was it, he thought, finding a small table inside the restaurant. He was fatigued, and seeing things.

He ordered and ate steak and potatoes, his mind still in a whirl. That girl. He couldn't shake the sight and sound. He'd spent many harrowing hours in Lucy's company, protecting her, beginning when he'd rescued her, through the fearful gun battle in the old church, to their two-day trip back to Carson City. He knew her well—her look, her gestures, the sound of her voice and her laughter. He'd bet all the money he had left that the girl passing down the street in the buggy was Lucinda Barkley. It was improbable that she'd be here, but he couldn't dismiss what he'd seen. But why? And hanging on the arm of a notorious character like Sam Stonehouse? There was no explaining it. The bullet wound in her calf must not be bothering her. But her long dress could have easily concealed a bandage on her leg.

He sighed and reached into a pocket for coins to pay for his meal he'd hardly tasted. His hand bumped his holstered Colt, and he glanced at the revolver. In spite of his efforts to keep it clean and functioning, dust and grit coated the cylinder and had gotten into the mechanism. He'd go back to his rooming house and clean the weapon thoroughly. There was no point in wearing a gun if it wasn't clean and oiled, ready for use at all times. The afternoon was far spent. If he could stay awake long enough, he'd make the rounds of the saloons and dance halls tonight. With a dozen or more theaters in town, Lucy and Sam might have gone to one of them. Or, they might not be in town at all.

But, knowing Samuel Stonehouse, Marc would bet he'd be found somewhere at the gaming tables. If Lucy *was* in Virginia

City with Stonehouse, Marc would find and confront her to learn what was going on.

CHAPTER 2

The sun edged above the horizon, forcing Lucinda Barkley to close her gritty eyes. She'd had no sleep all night, and her head fell forward as she dozed on the jouncing buckboard seat.

She jerked awake and grabbed the iron rail on the edge of the seat to keep from tumbling off.

"You better snap out of it, gal," the man beside her said. "We got a long way to go yet." He jerked a thumb over his shoulder at the bed of the wagon. "Go lay down back there awhile and catch some shut-eye. I'm used to staying up all night at the blackjack tables so I'm not tired yet. I'll let you relieve me in a couple hours." He shot her a glance from under the brim of his black hat. "Forgot to ask if you can drive a span o' mules."

"I'll learn quick enough," she rubbed her eyes. "No road in this desert, so what harm can I do?"

"Maybe go in big circles," the man replied. "But, I guess with daylight, you can guide by the sun. You said Lodestar is due east?"

"That's right. If we get anywhere close, we'll see it with the field glasses." She brushed a strand of hair out of her face and tucked it under her hat. She knew she must be a sight, but doubted her disheveled appearance and puffy eyes were of any concern to her companion. Sam Stonehouse, one of Virginia City's better-known gamblers, was on a single-minded quest for quick riches.

"Think I will lie down a few minutes," she said. During the

hours of cool darkness, she'd remained alert. But the moment the sun appeared, her whole body seemed to sag. She climbed over the seat and found a twenty-pound sack of shelled corn for a pillow. It was hard and coarse, but at least kept her head off the bouncing boards of the wagon. She lay down on her back, hat over her face.

Weakened by fatigue, she began to wonder if she'd acted too hastily. There'd been no time to pick and choose and evaluate. The decision had to be quick, and she'd made it. Her judgment of men wasn't always accurate. She had to find a man who was unattached, not too scrupulous, unemployed or with a chancy occupation, someone fairly intelligent and willing to take a risky gamble.

Those requirements eliminated most of the men she knew in Virginia City. She'd approached Sam Stonehouse the previous afternoon after watching him lose several hundred dollars at the faro layout in a Washoe saloon. She knew him by reputation only.

"Mister Stonehouse, I'm Lucinda Barkley," she'd said as he backed away from the faro table, a grim look on his face.

"So?" He moved away toward the bar, as if shooing off a bothersome fly. He grabbed a stoneware mug from the bar and helped himself to a cup of hot coffee from a silver urn. "Cream and sugar, Jerry!" he called to the bartender.

Lucy read desperation in his abrupt manner. From questioning the saloon girls, she discovered Sam drank very little, and not at all when gambling. She also found out he had no apparent interest in prostitutes and wasn't married or otherwise attached. Gambling and money seemed to be his only passions.

It was still early afternoon, but she had no time to lose.

She put her foot on the brass rail and leaned against the bar next to him. "Sam, I know a way you can recoup your losses many times over," she began quietly. The mid-afternoon business was slow and no one was within earshot.

"What'd you say your name was?"

"Lucinda Barkley . . . Lucy. I was the one kidnapped during that prison break down in Carson a few weeks back."

"Oh? Well, I'm glad to see you're back safe. What can I do for you?" He stirred the cream and sugar into his mug.

"I need the help of a strong, decisive man," she began.

He looked at her with interest for the first time. "Tell me about it."

His gray eyes never wavered from her as he listened with a gambler's patience while she briefly related her Lodestar adventure. She was careful not to disclose the exact location of the gold buried in the ruins of the church.

"That's a pretty wild story. How come I haven't heard about this?"

"I got home only this morning, and it hasn't hit the newspapers yet. By tomorrow or the day after, Ezra Pitney or Marc Charvein or the sheriff will probably have it spread across the pages of *The Territorial Enterprise,* the *Gold Hill News* and all the papers in Virginia City."

The handsome Stonehouse smiled, smoothing the ends of his sweeping mustache. "So . . . a lady with a pretty face, but a larcenous heart."

She felt her face burn with indignation. "I was kidnapped, starved, tied up, dragged on horseback across the desert, suffered from thirst, was shot at and wounded in the leg. I even saved a man's life at the end. Yet, what did I receive in return? Nothing. Not a penny. If no one will offer me any compensation for all that, then I'll just have to help myself, won't I?"

He nodded. "Where in Lodestar is this gold?"

"In a safe place, but it's too complicated to explain. I'll have to show you. If you help me get it, we'll split it evenly. What do you say?"

He blew on his hot coffee and took a sip, staring through the plate glass window into the street.

"If you decide against it, we'll just forget we had this conversation. I think I can rely on your discretion."

"Actually, you know nothing about me. I might blab this all over the city and go to the newspapers." He seemed to be suppressing a grin.

"I doubt you'd do that."

He was silent for a long minute. "How much gold did you say was left there?"

"I heard them say about a hundred pounds."

"So that'd be fifty apiece. Hmm . . . at current price of twenty-one dollars an ounce, that's roughly . . ."

For a man used to memorizing cards as they were played, he should be able to calculate this figure, she thought.

"Nearly $17,000," he said.

"Afterward, we'd have to go our separate ways, and not show up here again," she said.

"I've about played out my string of luck here, anyway."

"So you'll go?"

"When do we start?"

"As soon as it's dark tonight." She was relieved. "We have no time to lose. Ezra Pitney's been missing his gold for about five years, and he's gone to considerable trouble to recover most of what's left. I'd bet he won't waste time starting for Lodestar—probably tomorrow. But we have to take a couple shovels, a pick and maybe a pry bar."

"So it's buried?"

"It's well hidden. But we have to get there before Pitney." She glanced around and lowered her voice still further. "I have no money. We need a wagon, two mules, water and food and grain for the animals, a coil of stout rope. Maybe two light cavalry saddles for the mules if we split up."

"You have this all figured out, don't you?"

"I've been thinking about it for a couple of days."

"I have enough money left to outfit us. I'll trade my buggy and the Morgan." He glanced at her dress, then at his own black suit. "We'd best get into some clothes for desert travel. Then for a good supper and we're off at the rising of the moon."

Lucy sat up in the buckboard. The jarring made it impossible to sleep. They really should have bought a spring wagon, but Stonehouse was trying to save money.

She dug out the binoculars from one of the packs. But scanning the entire horizon ahead showed nothing but a wasteland of sand, caked gray mud of a dry playa, short rows of low desert mountains. Probably another 30 miles, she guessed. No use trying to hurry it. Walking and trotting, the mules would cover a lot of ground, but Stonehouse dared not push the animals, or she and the gambler would be afoot. The early September heat showed no signs of coming autumn, so a rest and water stop would be in order soon. There was no shade anywhere.

Later that afternoon, Lucy fell asleep in the wagon out of sheer exhaustion and slept for two hours. She relieved Sam at the reins just before sundown and drove until it was nearly too dark to see when they stopped for the night. They camped within walking distance of a low mountain range. Enough brush grew on its slopes for a campfire.

Stonehouse gathered several armloads of small dry sticks and greasewood, just enough to boil some coffee and cook. They unhitched the mules. Lucy rubbed them down with an old blanket, wiping off the crusted salt. Relieved of their sweaty harness, the animals rolled in the dust, then directed their attention to the grain and water buckets. "Take care of them and they'll take care of us," Stonehouse muttered as he squatted down and struck a match to the pile of brush.

The night chill crept in over the high desert and Lucy sat close to the fire for warmth and cheer. During the day the sun had been her enemy, but the tiny fire was her friend at night.

They dug into their supplies. Lucy wasn't used to camping out in the wild, but after watching and helping Charvein, she now hoped to give the impression she wasn't just a protected city girl. She used two small rocks to crush a double handful of coffee beans to boil. She'd remembered to bring a "spider" and set the small iron tripod with a flat top over the flames to hold the coffeepot. Later, as Stonehouse stirred a small pot of beans and turned sizzling bacon, Lucy glanced toward the west where the sun was going down in a welter of crimson and gold.

Before they left town, Lucy had changed into a canvas riding skirt that reached well below her knees. Her boots hid the bandaged calf wound, but didn't hide her perceptible limp. If Stonehouse noticed, he didn't comment. If she kept the wound clean, it should heal with no problem. So as not to appear vulnerable, she didn't want Stonehouse to know the extent of her injury. If he should demand some proof of her story, she could then reveal the bullet wound. *Don't show even a hint of weakness around this man,* she told herself. He wasn't trustworthy. No gambler was. Yet he was the only man available, and she'd been lucky to entice him with this hasty venture.

During their break from the Carson City prison, the two escapees had taken her hostage, confiscating the derringer Lucy's father had given her when she went to work in the prison warden's office. After returning home, she'd removed a small Smith and Wesson from a cabinet in her father's study, along with a box of .38 cartridges. The weapon hadn't been touched in years, and her father would likely never miss it. She'd cleaned the gun and wiped the verdigris off the brass cartridges, hoping they were still good.

She'd greeted her parents warmly, and her mother fixed a hearty meal of pancakes. While they ate, Lucy briefed them on her adventure and finished by saying she'd be going to Virginia City right away and would be in touch with them later. She referred vaguely to meeting Charvein and leaving an affidavit with the sheriff about the violent events in Lodestar.

After the meal, her father dropped her off at her own little house near the train depot. By mid-afternoon, she'd bathed, cleaned and re-bandaged her leg wound, changed clothes, taken what little money she had and caught the train to Virginia City, several miles north. Her plan was underway.

Her parents were still concerned, but recognized her independence and the fact that, at age twenty-seven, she had to make a life for herself. They were just thankful to have her back, nearly unscathed.

With the going of the sun, she pulled up closer to the fire, wrapping her arms around her knees. The flames were now their only source of light. She recalled how black it was at night in Lodestar until the town caught fire or the moon rose.

Stonehouse served up the smoking bacon and beans on two tin plates and handed one across to her. She set a cup of coffee on a rock beside her and they began to eat. He didn't speak. She assumed he was a taciturn man by nature, as well as profession. She could only guess what he was thinking. With night, would he assume he was going to sleep with her? They were barely acquainted strangers. The loaded Smith & Wesson with the four-inch barrel was securely tucked into her waistband under her jacket. She would actively discourage any such ideas—if she could stay awake.

They should reach Lodestar by tomorrow afternoon. How far behind was Ezra Pitney? He and his men were surely coming quickly. She'd never met Pitney but knew his reputation for greed. A wealthy man, he wanted more, ever more. Public speculation by Pitney's enemies in Virginia City indicated he could never get enough to make up for the iron-claw poverty of his youth.

Judging from his manner all day, she thought Stonehouse considered this jaunt a lark. How could she convince him otherwise? Perhaps a casual, devil-may-care attitude was a demeanor that gamblers assumed.

They finished eating and scrubbed their dishes and utensils with clean sand to save precious water.

With a burning twig, Stonehouse lit a slim cigar and then squinted at her through the tobacco and wood smoke.

"Well, Miss Lucy, here we are. We've been on the trail for a night and a day, and I'm about tuckered out. But we haven't much farther to go."

"You won't regret throwing in with me," she ground her teeth at being called "Miss Lucy." It made her sound like a prim old maid.

Could she trust Sam to deal with her fairly? Or would he rape and kill her and ride off with all the plunder after they found it? Given her active imagination, she had trouble controlling these wild thoughts. *Proceed as planned,* she thought. *But keep a wary eye on his every move.* What about his ability, or willingness, to camp in the desert and perform hard physical labor digging gold out of the rubble of the collapsed church?

Even though he was lean and appeared to be in good condition for a man of forty or so, Sam Stonehouse had the soft hands of a gambler and might be averse to working like a miner.

She sipped her coffee and looked over the rim of the tin cup at him. She'd apparently caught him at a good time—in the midst of a long streak of bad luck when he was amenable to her proposition of gold for the taking, untraceable gold that had been melted into a different form, all stampings of the original owner removed from the ingots.

Her impulsive expedition had the thrill of danger and made her tingle with delicious fear. It was like the dangerous age of long ago when knights and ladies and brigands peopled Europe. She chose to ignore what must have been unsanitary living conditions prevailing centuries ago, along with early death from disease. By standards of those times, she'd have been, at age 27, a spinster on the verge of middle age.

She thought of the gun battles in Lodestar and the dynamited church. She mentally transformed that experience into the defense of a medieval castle. Charvein became an armorless knight coming to her rescue. And then she'd returned the favor by saving him. Yes, maybe there wasn't much difference between then and now. People still moved about with horses and carriages, and did much the same things, except for weapons and mode of dress. Of course, the code of chivalry was different.

She came out of her reverie to see Sam's black eyes watching her from across the campfire. For some reason, she thought of a rattler eyeing a kangaroo rat. She swallowed and looked away into the darkness.

What was that? A tiny pinprick of light out there in a sea of black. Then it was gone, and she wasn't sure she'd even seen it. Her stomach tensed. Ezra Pitney might be closer than she thought.

CHAPTER 3

An hour later, Lucy wrapped herself in a blanket, slipped off her boots and lay down, feet toward the coals of the dying fire.

Stonehouse slept beneath the wagon, but Lucy still kept her .38 close at hand under her rolled-up jacket that functioned as a pillow. The gambler propped his head on one of the two McClellan saddles they'd brought and soon was snoring quietly.

Though not soft, the sandy soil allowed her to burrow out a couple of shallow depressions that conformed to her body. In spite of any night-crawling insects, the ground was still a lot better than the hard boards of the wagon and had even retained some of the warmth of the sun.

Though exhausted, she couldn't fall asleep right away, and lay awake listening to Sam's steady breathing several yards away. She was relieved he had no apparent interest in her.

Finally she dozed, but didn't sleep soundly.

Sometime later, the cold woke her. She curled into a ball under the blanket. A bright moon was shining. She heard Sam snort and turn over in his sleep. Unable to shiver herself warm, she sat up and pulled on her jacket and boots. She pressed a hand gently to the bandage on her calf. A little sore. Probably healing.

A wisp of smoke curled up in the windless air from the dead campfire. The night was still. She got up and quietly moved to the wagon, took the field glasses and scanned the dimly lit landscape, focusing on their backtrail. The foreshortened

24

distance finally blurred into darkness. She moved the glasses slightly—and caught her breath. A tiny pinpoint of light shone steadily. How far away? No telling. Did the people around that campfire also have a spyglass or binoculars? She should have thought to be watching their backtrail during daylight, perhaps to catch a glimpse of whoever was following. Pitney? She knew the mine owner wouldn't send his hired help to retrieve the gold; he'd come himself, even if he brought a couple of men. All traces of a road to the former boomtown had long since been obliterated by wind and dust. But her and Sam's wagon tracks would be visible. Would they travel by wagon? More likely by horseback, trailing at least one pack mule. If so, they'd have to be toting water kegs and grain for the animals.

On their way home from Lodestar to Carson City, Marc Charvein had told her about *tinajas*—tanks. The low desert mountains contained huge granite boulders, some with hollows scoured out by eons of wind and sand storms. The hollows collected rainwater in season. These gamey waterholes were a lifesaver for desert travelers. She and Charvein had looked for them. The only scummy pool they'd found was nearly dry.

She lowered the glasses. It wasn't likely the builders of that campfire were merely chance travelers or prospectors. Charvein told her that even the Indians avoided this region during the driest months because the *tinajas* were not dependable. Whoever was out there had a reason for traveling this way. And she had a good idea what that was.

Time to go. Her mules and buckboard had left a trail as easy to follow as a railroad track. Her only hope lay in stretching the distance and buying time.

She tucked her pistol under her waistband, walked to the buckboard where Sam lay sleeping and nudged him with the toe of her boot.

"Sam! Wake up."

He stirred.

"Sam!"

"Huh? What?" He rolled over.

"Get up. We have to go."

"Why?" He propped up on his elbow. "What time is it?"

"Maybe three o'clock."

"Go back to sleep. I'm eager to get there, too. But we have to rest the mules and ourselves."

"There's a campfire behind us. I think Pitney's following."

Without a word, Sam rolled to his feet, flinging off the blanket. He reached for his gunbelt and hat. "Gimme the binoculars."

He silently searched the direction she pointed.

"Hmmm . . ." He handed the binoculars back. "Before we take the hobbles off the mules, give them each a small bucket of water with flour poured into it to make a slurry. That'll give 'em strength. We'll save their nosebags and grain for later."

While Lucy hurried to obey, Sam pulled on his short jacket against the night chill and scuffed dirt over the remains of the campfire, then sorted the harness by moonlight.

Within a half-hour, they were hitched up and on their way.

"The moon's just past full. It'll still be high in the sky after daylight. We can cover a lot of ground at a slow pace while it's cool and the mules won't have to work so hard."

Lucy knew this, but let him talk. He was a stranger to her, but it was comforting to hear another human voice in this vast void of space.

She chewed on a dry biscuit and sipped water from a canteen, hardly aware of eating. Every few seconds, she scanned the horizon behind them until the tiny point of light was no longer visible. *Why didn't I pay more attention to the distance and pace when Marc and I were returning from Lodestar?* she thought. She'd been so relieved to be free of danger and in the hands of someone trustworthy, she hardly stopped talking the whole two days.

They would gain at least another four or five hours on their pursuers. She knew Sam was resisting the urge to hurry. Slow but steady would win this race. Their pursuers—if that's what they were—had to cover the same ground under the same conditions.

She hadn't had enough sleep. And once they hit Lodestar, there would be no sleep until after they'd recovered the gold and left. The steady clopping of the mules and gentle motion of the buckboard eased her tension, and she felt her shoulders droop. She slept, slumped on the hard seat, swaying with the wagon's movement, her subconscious still alert enough to catch her if she began to fall. Not good rest, but at least it was rest.

When she again opened her eyes, the world was gray; a red streak stained the horizon ahead. She sat up, rolling her head to relieve the crick in her neck.

"Grab the glasses and take a look up yonder," Sam said.

She reached into the wagon for the binoculars and focused them. A mile or more ahead, at the base of a short jumble of mountains, she could make out traces of buildings. Atop the low mountain to the right she saw the tiny outline of a building, and recognized it for the tin shed that housed the head frame of a mineshaft. Her stomach tensed. It was the same building where she and Charvein and Sandoval were held prisoner during their ordeal.

This second visit to Lodestar stirred a lot of unpleasant memories. But she was determined to put all that behind her and concentrate on their purpose here. This time she'd help herself to the compensation she was due for what she'd endured.

CHAPTER 4

Marc Charvein made the rounds of several popular saloons and gambling halls the night he spotted Lucinda Barkley and gambler Sam Stonehouse in the buggy together. But he found neither of them.

Maybe I'll see her later, he thought on his way back to his boardinghouse after midnight. It was idle curiosity only. He had no claim on the girl with whom he'd shared the wild adventure in Lodestar. They'd saved each other's lives, and that was the end of it. Things were even. With nothing in common, they'd go their separate ways. Although they hadn't discussed it during their time together, he'd found her physically attractive, with a pleasant personality, though something of a dreamer. And he knew she was drawn to him as well. Or was she just dependent on him to bring her home safely from the ordeal and the danger of a wild gun battle?

He thought of her fondly—probably why he'd felt a pang of jealousy to see her with another man so soon after their return. But now it was time to put her in the past and move on with his life. If he ever encountered her again, it would probably be by happenstance.

Next morning, rested and refreshed, Charvein made a decision. He'd leave Virginia City and go south to the Arizona Territory to spend the coming winter in a warmer, desert climate. He had no ties here. His only living relatives—aunts, uncles and several cousins—were still east of the Mississippi. He thought he could stretch his money long enough to find a job of some sort down south.

Once he made the decision to start anew elsewhere, he still had a little unfinished business. He went to the sheriff's office to turn in his badge and temporary deputy's commission.

While there, he gave the same abbreviated version of the story he'd told Pitney.

"Denson Boyd's two partners showed up here in custody of the posse." Sheriff Dan Farmer fingered the worn badge Charvein handed him. "I've got 'em in a cell waiting for a marshal to transport them back to prison at Carson City." He stood up and came around his desk. "The man heading up the posse told me some wild tale about Buck Rankin leaving them to fend for themselves in a dust storm, and later shooting Shooner. And Rankin hasn't shown up either. You know anything about all this? What actually happened out there in Lodestar?"

Charvein shrugged. "Don't know nothing about the doings of the posse, sheriff. But it looks like they brought back Boyd's two ex-partners. Why don't you ask them?"

"Oh, they'll be questioned thoroughly, right enough. One of them's got a bad arm wound. The doc from the prison will be over to look at it soon. It looks to be mortified. If he dies, we'll have only the testimony of the other one. Of course, the posse men told me only bits and pieces."

"I reported to Ezra Pitney yesterday. Told him where to find his gold. He paid me off and we're quits."

"Yeah, he told me he was taking a couple of men and heading out that way early this morning."

"Right," Charvein said. "Well, I'm off. Have a lot of things to catch up on."

"Stay close by. Might need you if a coroner's jury is convened."

"I'll be around for a short time, but I have business down south in the Territory." Charvein nodded pleasantly and walked out the door, leaving Sheriff Farmer scowling behind him.

If anything would have spurred him to hasten his departure from Virginia City, it was the sight of the disbelieving sheriff. Charvein was glad he'd dropped the comment about leaving for the Territory. He had no desire to get entangled in some legal investigation that would not really change anything and could drag out for weeks, going off on various tangents. To his thinking, everything had been resolved and dredging up details would serve no purpose.

He went to his boarding house, packed his few clothes and personal articles into his saddlebags, then walked to the livery stable to claim the mule he'd ridden in on—one that'd belonged to the late Denson Boyd. Charvein felt the mule was rightfully his, since Boyd had shot and killed Charvein's horse in an ambush. Charvein had left Boyd's other mule with Lucy in Carson City. Within a block of the stable, a thought struck him and he stopped in the middle of the boardwalk. He had no proof this mule belonged to him. No bill of sale. It was only a spoil of war and had been ridden by Denson Boyd, one of the outlaws. Maybe it was best he not be seen riding an animal with someone else's brand. For all he knew the mule might've been stolen.

Should he leave the mule to be eventually claimed by the livery owner for non-payment of a boarding bill? Only if he planned to stay in town, he thought. As long as he was leaving, he'd chance riding this hardy mule. Long gaps in the rail line existed between here and the southern desert, and he didn't want to depend on riding a train. A good mount was a better option.

"Well, did you take good care of my mule?" he asked as he entered the stable.

"Yeah, but he's been rode hard," the liveryman said. "Got a couple of galls on his back. He could probably use some more rest and feed."

Charvein hadn't really paid much attention to the condition of the mule on their ride back from Lodestar, but realized the pack animal had endured nearly as much as the humans during the Lodestar ordeal.

"You in the market for a mule?" Charvein asked suddenly, reaching over the stall door and rubbing the animal's white nose.

"I might."

"I'm leaving town. Need a horse that has good bottom for a long trip. Maybe we can work out a trade."

"Hmmm . . . I got a nice one over here. Cross between a mustang and a Morgan. Not big, but hardy."

The livery owner didn't ask for a bill of sale and Charvein traded the mule and cash for the black. From his limited knowledge of horseflesh, he was satisfied with the deal.

Next day he spent preparing to leave. He invested in an oversize set of saddlebags and stuffed them with dried beef, dried fruit, beans and bread, along with a frying pan and other utensils. When he retrieved his newly acquired horse from the livery, he traded his heavy saddle to the owner for an old, deep-seated California saddle that was 13 pounds lighter. Then he used his sheath knife to trim away all unnecessary leather to lighten it still further.

The second set of saddlebags contained a change of clothing, razor, personal items and matches coated with wax for waterproofing. Anticipating having to chop firewood, he even added a hatchet. His main concern was water. There was no way he could carry enough for himself and his mount. He'd have to ride from spring to spring, and stay within range of the few rivers and year-round streams. But he bought a leather water bag for emergencies. Filled, it was heavy and bulky, but he couldn't take a chance of running dry in the Nevada desert in early September. He thought of waiting for cooler autumn days and eventually the early winter rains, but didn't think his money would last that long. Finally, he stowed a rolled-up blanket and slicker behind the cantle.

One last item he debated about buying. Should he keep his old, worn Colt .45 that had served him well for years? He was familiar with all its idiosyncrasies. It didn't lock up as tight as it used to. Perhaps it was time for something new and different—a new weapon for his fresh start.

"Looks like you got your money's worth out of this one," Curt Gunterson said when Charvein handed over his old Colt at the Virginia City gunshop. "Take a look at what I have here."

Charvein scanned the display case of new and used handguns. Nothing caught his eye; all he saw were too small, too large, or too expensive. He'd often envisioned the ideal pistol—large enough caliber to do some damage, but not so powerful the recoil would be bothersome; barrel long enough to be accurate, but short enough to carry comfortably; easy availability of ammunition.

"Got anything else?" he asked without much hope.

"Actually, just received two new Merwin Hulberts today," Gunterson said. "Haven't had time to put them out."

"I've heard of those."

"Probably the best-made gun I've ever seen," he replied. "And they're the third largest-selling pistol behind Colt and Remington. Wait a minute." Gunterson vanished into the back room and reappeared with two boxes he set on the counter.

"This .32 has interchangeable barrels," he pointed out. "Here's how it works." He pushed a button under the frame, twisted the barrel and slid it forward, released a catch and the four-inch barrel and cylinder came off. He quickly replaced it with the six-inch barrel, clicking it into place. "Cartridge rims catch under the edge and are pulled out when the cylinder slides forward. The empties drop out and any unfired cartridges stay in because they're longer."

"Very unusual." He took the proffered grip and thumbed back the hammer. "Good, tight feel to it."

"Mostly hand-fitted, they tell me. And nearly all models come from the factory just as you see—nickel-plated with pearl or ivory grips at no extra charge." He opened the second box. "Also have a single-action .44 model with an open top frame."

Charvein examined them both and compared their weight and feel. "I like the .32, but I'd prefer a .38, if you have it."

"Sorry. I could special-order one for you."

"Never mind. Won't be here that long. I'll take the .32 with both barrels. And three boxes of ammunition."

"You won't be sorry. I'll knock off some on the price for your old Colt." Gunterson put the weapon back into the box.

Charvein reached for gold coin to pay. He was intrigued by the idea of the interchangeable barrels and the different design. He could carry the shorter weapon, but would have the longer-range one available at any time. It was like buying two guns for the price of one.

"Where ya headed?" Gunterson asked.

"South. Arizona Territory."

"What route?"

Charvein shrugged. "Don't know. Probably cross directly southeast."

"Some hellish, dry country between here and there. There's a good reason that area's known as Furnace Creek and Death Valley."

"You've been down that way?"

"Yeah. Used to have a shop in Tombstone, until the town

started to settle down. Plenty of business here, though, while things are still booming."

"What's the best route to the Territory?"

Gunterson didn't hesitate. "Ride south past Carson to Aurora, Nevada. Then cut west to Bodie, California, just across the line. Work your way down through the mountains. You and your horse might be able to hitch a ride on a freight train part of the way. The mountains will be slower going, but there's water and forage—and it's cooler."

"You have a map by chance?"

"No, but you might be able to buy one in Carson City, or at one of the railroad depots."

"Great. Thanks. I'm doubly glad I stopped in here." He hefted the sack with the boxed gun and extra cartridges. "Almost forgot. I need a new holster to fit this new . . . new Merwin Hulbert. That name's a mouthful. Not like the word 'Colt.' Think I'll just call it my Merwin."

"Or *Merlin,* like the magician," the gunsmith said.

Charvein chuckled as he unbuckled his old gunbelt and dropped it on the counter.

"I don't have a belt with cartridge loops for the smaller .32."

"Never mind. Just give me the holster and I'll wear it on my regular belt."

An hour later, he was in the saddle and headed south for Carson City.

CHAPTER 5

"It's hotter'n the iron hub of Hades!" Sam Stonehouse dropped the pick. Its steel point clanged against a large stone on the pile of rubble that had been San Juan Church. He stepped toward the buckboard, swabbing his face with a blue bandanna. "Gimme that canteen."

Lucy tossed it to him. He pulled the cork and tilted it up, taking several large swallows, his Adam's apple working up and down. "Ahh . . ." He capped the container. "It's warm but at least it's wet."

Lucy stood looking westward over the heaps of blackened timbers that had once been a row of wooden buildings on one side of the street. She could see directly to the west, across the dry mud of a wide, shallow playa. It was past ten in the morning, but there was no sign of anyone.

Three hours earlier the wind had picked up and was now gusting from the northwest, blowing up dust, rattling pebbles against the warped walls of empty buildings. She started at every noise. Nerves and lack of sleep had put her on edge. "Better hurry," she called over the noise of the wind.

"See anybody?"

"Not yet. But they can't be too far behind."

"You wanta take a turn at this? Maybe we should both work, and it'll go faster."

"In a minute. Somebody has to keep watch. We don't want to be surprised by any visitors."

"Tell me again where you think this bell tower fell. And about where the altar would be."

Lucy walked over and looked. "The tower was just to the left of the front door, about here . . ." She pointed. "And the altar was way in the back of the church over there." She had trouble recalling how the place looked before several sticks of dynamite had blown out the walls and the roof came crashing down. It had been one of only two stone buildings in town. The other was the bank.

They'd seen no one in town, and the place had a dead feel, but in spite of her intuition that Sandoval was gone, Lucy wanted to make sure.

"I'll be back in a minute," she said.

"Where you goin'?" Sam sounded irritated. "Don't go wandering off."

"A call of nature."

"Oh."

"I won't be long."

She walked quickly away toward the end of the sloping hill where a clump of trees hid the entrance to Sandoval's cave.

Once out of sight, she slipped into the hidden entrance. As she expected, the room was completely cleaned out. Even the manure had been swept outside. Carlos Sandoval had taken his animals, gear and supplies, leaving behind only a rusty lantern. She shook it and heard coal oil sloshing inside. Good. She wondered if he anticipated someone coming and using his dug-out mine tunnel. He'd kept his promise to leave, probably even before his arm wound was healed. The ashes of dead campfires and a firepit were evidence of his long occupation.

Several yards along the dark tunnel leading out the rear of the room was a vertical mineshaft filled with clear, cold water. Access to that water had been the key to Sandoval's survival here. She wondered if he would've stayed several years if there'd been no gold to find. She suspected he'd chosen to linger here for two reasons: One was to allow plenty of time for the law to lose interest in looking for him. The other was his desire to be near the desert grave of the wife he'd accidentally shot while she was being raped by Deputy Marshal Buck Rankin. Rankin, himself, now occupied a new grave in the town cemetery. Lucy could only guess what Sandoval must have suffered during those long months of lonely vigil. She shook her head and heaved a sigh. But now it was her turn to take a share of the gold.

She returned to the ruined church where Stonehouse was still turning over rocks. He'd managed to work his way down about two feet into the pile.

"There's that damned bell! I can just see the top of it. Looks like brass, though."

"It's only the two clappers inside that're made of gold," Lucy bent to brush the dust and plaster off the top of the bell.

"Now, if I can just get this thing out of here . . ." he muttered, tearing at the surrounding rocks and wood splinters with gloved hands.

Lucy resumed watching their backtrail. It was still empty.

The mules were hobbled in the shade with buckets of water near them. She'd put some grain in their nosebags earlier.

Several minutes later she heard Sam swear. She glanced up.

"Got it!" He dragged the bell into the street, the clappers clanking. He dashed to the buckboard and grabbed a pair of wire cutters. A minute later he'd snipped the wire that fastened the clappers to the inside of the bell. Using both arms, he carried one of the gold clappers to the wagon. "Stash that in a canvas bag."

He returned for the second clapper and heaved it into the wagon. "Well, little lady, you weren't lying," he panted, leaning on the side of the buckboard, his face streaked with white where the sweat had dried in the hot wind.

"That's just part of it. The rest is under the altar, Sandoval said."

"Who said?"

"The old desert rat I told you about. The one who discovered the gold and made these bell clappers."

"Is it still in ingots?"

Lucy shook her head. "I never saw it, but he said he cast it in the form of a cross when he didn't have the skill to make a bell."

Stonehouse straightened up with a groan. "Damn! Now I know why I never did manual labor for a living. Those miners earn every penny they're paid."

He clapped his hat on, hefted the pick and spade and went back to work, taking one of the full canteens with him.

Lucy ducked her face away from a gust of wind. Fine grit was being driven into every inch of her exposed skin. She didn't recall it being this bad when she was here the week before, but then survival had been on her mind and she was hardly aware of the weather.

She walked slowly to the end of the street, noting all the familiar sights that were branded into her memory—the rusted pump in the middle of the street, the bank building with its stone entrance, the false fronts on the stores and the old two-story hotel, with its broken windows and sagging front porch.

I wonder what this town looked like when it was booming, she thought. But, in spite of the mental effort, she couldn't picture it full of people, horses, mules and wagons with the thumping of stamp mills, and wide-open saloons blaring their raucous clatter into the street.

It was only a relic now, plaything of the sand and wind and rain—natural elements slowly breaking it down to what it had been before any precious metal was discovered here.

A distant rumble startled her and she looked back toward

Virginia City. The playa was empty. Then she saw thunderheads building over the mountain range to the northwest. She studied the towering white clouds and their dark bases for a few moments, but dismissed them as a promise that would remain unfulfilled. Sandoval had told them thunderstorms often muttered and grumbled over the western mountains. But rarely did any rain make it to Lodestar, except in certain seasons, when storms from the distant Pacific drove moisture over the low ranges into the interior of Nevada. For now, the dry playas would remain just that—dry, shallow lakebeds.

After a last look at their backtrail with the binoculars, she returned to the ruins where Stonehouse was still digging.

Since there was no one in sight, Lucy decided to pitch in and help. Sam looked as if he was wearing down. She pulled on a pair of gloves and began pitching smaller rocks and shingles aside.

Sam stood up and wiped a sleeve across his brow. "Part of the ridgepole beam fell right where you said the altar was located," he said. "Both of us together can't move that. It still has part of the roof attached."

He was right. "Good thing we brought those coils of rope," she said. "Maybe we can't move that big piece, but let's dig around it as much as we can, and then we'll hitch up the mules and let them drag it out of the way."

"Good thinking, gal," Sam grinned. "Keep pulling the small stuff from around it and find me a good place to attach the ropes. I'll go hitch up the mules. They been resting for a few hours. They oughta be up to the job. If they can't do it, we'll have to figure out something else."

While he was dealing with the animals, Lucy made sure the beam and the section of roof weren't attached to anything larger.

Sam returned, leading the mules in their collars and harness. He rigged double loops of rope to each harness, backed the animals into position and secured the rope ends to the wooden roof beams.

"All right." He took hold of the reins and stood to one side. "Hiyah! Giddap!" He popped the long lines over their backs and the mules threw their weight into the breast bands. The slack tightened and the rope began to vibrate as they dug in their hooves. Slowly, the beam and its attached section of roof pivoted slightly off the pile and began to slide.

"That's it!" Lucy cried. "Just a little more."

"Whoa!" Sam halted the team. "That's got it. What's underneath? We still need the mules?"

"Looks okay. Just small stuff from here."

Sam guided the team into the shade, but left them in harness. He rejoined Lucy and the two of them began to dig furiously.

Sweat stung her eyes, and her hair fell across her face, but she didn't bother with any of that. She knew they had to hurry. If those following had started at daybreak and traveled steadily, they would be here before dark. If those traveling behind were the ones she suspected, she and Sam had to retrieve the gold and be away before night. They couldn't afford to be seen, even from a distance, or they'd likely be caught. A city-soft gambler, a woman and two tired mules pulling a buckboard would be run down and shot or arrested. Except for the intermittent low desert mountain ranges, there was no place in the vicinity to hide. She never doubted the distant firelight she'd seen belonged to Pitney. Certainly no one else would have any reason to be out here.

Then a thought struck her—could it be Marc Charvein? Maybe he hadn't gone to report to Ezra Pitney, but had only stopped overnight in Virginia City, bought a fresh horse and supplies and headed straight back here to dig out the treasure for himself? But she immediately dismissed the idea. She fancied herself a good judge of people. Charvein was a totally different kind of man than Sam Stonehouse. In her estimation, Charvein was a man of integrity and courage. He would not stoop to theft, would not cross the man who'd hired him. But, then, she'd seen gold fever corrupt even the most honest of men.

While this was playing out in her mind, she was bent over the jumble of rock, shingles and splintered boards, flinging away small chunks as fast as she could.

Sam fell in beside her and they worked wordlessly and steadily. Her back began to ache and she stood up and stretched. Then she got down on her knees and dug with her hands. There was no need for a shovel or a pick. It was all loose debris now.

They paused after fifteen minutes for a long drink out of two canteens.

"I hope we brought plenty of water," Sam capped the metal container and shook it. "This one's about empty. And the mules are sure sucking up the water from those kegs mighty fast."

Lucy nodded. She knew they had no worries about water, but didn't want to reveal the source of the unlimited sweet water in the mineshaft just yet. She wasn't sure why. But, like the gambler she was dealing with, she wouldn't show all her cards until she had to.

Before she resumed digging, she hurried down the street a block and took another long look with the binoculars. In spite of the dry, clear air, the far distance seemed fuzzy, obscured by a haze. She looked without the glasses, then refocused them. Blowing dust. The wind forcing the thunderheads toward Lodestar was also whipping along the ground, roiling up fine powder from the surface of the playa.

She put the glasses away, thinking she surely had no desire to experience another one of those ferocious dust storms. Another reason they had to hurry. With any luck, the approaching wind might delay or stall Pitney and his men. She had seen only their firelight, but she was as certain of their presence as if she'd been conversing with them.

"Let's get moving," she rejoined Sam and pulled on her leather gloves.

"Somebody coming?"

She nearly smiled at his startled look. Disheveled hair, wide eyes and sunburned nose above the mustache made him look like a clown with makeup.

"No people. Dust storm headed this way. Storm clouds, too, but I'm not worried about those."

He resumed digging with the shovel, heaving showers of powdery plaster and small stones downwind.

The point of his shovel thudded on something solid. "Oh! Guess we need the mules again."

Lucy sprang down into the depression and began brushing the dust away. "No. This is it—part of the altar. See the polished rosewood? Different from the pine floor or pews." She pointed. "And look here . . ." She was growing more excited. If Sandoval had told the truth, they were very close. "Here's the altar stone."

"What's that?"

"A flat stone set in the center of the altar. Contains tiny relics of one or more saints."

"Huh?"

"An old tradition. When the first-century Christians were being hunted and killed by the Romans, they went underground to say Mass in the catacombs and usually set up an altar on the top of a flat grave containing the bones of someone who'd been martyred for the faith."

While she answered him, both were busy digging around the edges of the altar top.

"I'll fetch the mules," Sam grunted. "This thing's too heavy for us."

Several minutes later, the team was again tied to the heavy, half-buried slab of rosewood, and Sam eased them forward, dragging the wood out of the pile.

"Here it is!" Lucy said.

Sam halted the team, dropped the reins and scrambled back to see a wooden dynamite box with the lid askew. He reached with a shovel and pushed the top off. Inside lay a few broken lumps of pure gold, along with a slightly crooked gold cross.

"Just like he told us," Lucy said.

"By God!" Stonehouse lay flat on the pile and stretched one arm down into the enclosure, pulling up a handful of the small nuggets. He rolled them over in his palm before shoving them into a side pocket of his pants. Then he gripped one arm of the cross and tugged.

"Uh! Heavy!" He stood up and took a deep breath. "Can't lift it with one hand. Need some leverage." He reached into the hole with a pick and hooked one handle of the wooden box. Then he squatted, gripping the vertical pick handle with both hands, and stood, lifting the box and its contents and dragging it over the lip of the hole.

He dropped the pick and reached into the deep wooden box, pulling the rough-cast cross upright. It was two and a half to three feet tall with a cross arm about two-thirds of that. It gleamed softly in the sunlight. "Now, that's what I call a beauty!" He planted a kiss on the cross, then grinned at Lucy, teeth flashing white against his sunburned face.

A chill went over her at what she saw as sacrilege—kissing the cross not out of reverence, but out of greed.

He laid the cross back in the wooden box among the loose gold chips. She noted he didn't replace the few he'd pocketed.

Sam's eyes almost glowed. "How much, you reckon?"

Lucy shrugged. "We can weigh it later." She was surprised at her own neutral reaction. She thought she'd be more excited. Maybe it just hadn't hit her yet. She'd been so focused on retrieving the gold, she hadn't let herself dream of the things it would buy.

He heaved up the wooden box by both its rope handles and staggered toward the buckboard with his burden. He slid it onto the tailgate of the wagon. "Must weigh more than fifty pounds, I'd judge."

She glanced at the sky. The mid-afternoon sun was obscured. The white clouds were boiling ever higher, leaning toward them until it seemed the snowy pillars would avalanche down onto Lodestar, burying what remained of the old ghost town.

Lucy's stomach tensed, and it wasn't from any impending weather. She'd learned to trust her instincts, her intuition, her premonitions, or whatever these feelings were called. "Let's hurry."

Sam needed no urging. In spite of no food, little sleep, and hard physical labor most of the day in the hot sun, he seemed more energized than ever. Rubbing his hands together, he kept glancing toward the box and the clappers in the wagon bed. "A good stake to start fresh somewhere away from Virginia City!"

At the moment, Lucy was a bit numb. What had she expected? Did she think the gold would jump out of the pile and embrace her? It was simply yellow metal.

"We'll camp out in one of these vacant buildings," Sam said, "cook up a good meal and get some sleep. Then, tomorrow, we'll . . ." His voice trailed off.

Lucy had the binoculars to her eyes and caught her breath. The twin lenses picked out something moving far out on the other side of the playa. She turned the focus knob and looked more intently. Her eyes detected tiny figures moving out of the dusty haze. They were barely visible, like tiny black insects, but moving steadily in this direction. Five horsemen. No—only three, and trailing two animals. Either spare mounts or pack mules, she guessed.

She lowered the glasses. "Three riders coming."

CHAPTER 6

"What?" The grin disappeared. "Damn! Always a horsefly in the tapioca. I knew this was too easy." He looked to her, as if for direction.

"I told you they'd be coming. That's why we had to get the jump and be here first."

"Well, by God, we got the gold now, and I ain't giving it up."

She jerked a thumb at the sky. "Early for autumn downpours, but I'd guess we'll get a boomer tonight." She shrugged. "Unless I'm wrong, that blowing dust will be nearly as bad."

"What d'you suggest?" he asked. "We can't stay here. If we take off, they're sure to see us. I was hoping to get some sleep. I'm bone tired and sore."

"Hitch the team to the buckboard," Lucy said. "I know a place where they won't find us tonight."

She brought the glasses to her eyes again. A dark veil of rain was trailing from the leaden base of the clouds. She couldn't tell if it was reaching the ground. But it was sweeping toward them, overtaking the dust cloud. The riders were nowhere to be seen. They were either choking on dust or were being drenched by what Charvein had described as "male rain"—a pounding, torrential deluge from the black clouds.

Lucy had a plan, but it would require exact timing and stamina that perhaps neither of them had. If the plan failed, was she prepared to defend the gold with her life? She hoped she wouldn't have to find the answer to that. But the .38 in her

Cross of Gold

waistband and a hundred extra cartridges sagging her pocket comforted her. This situation was certainly a far cry from working in an office, but she thrilled at actually *living* and not just existing.

The wind out ahead of the storm front was beginning to gust, swirling around the street, blowing away the hoof prints and wheel marks they'd made. What about any fresh mule droppings? She didn't have time to search for those. She hoped the men who were coming weren't good enough trackers to distinguish between the signs of today and those of a few days earlier since everything was quickly being covered with dust.

Stonehouse finished hitching the mules to the wagon.

"This way. Hurry!" Lucy urged him.

Leading the team, he followed her toward the far end of the main street where the buildings dwindled away into the desert beyond. She circled the base of the sloping hill to a thick copse of trees. She halted, realizing the buckboard wouldn't fit between the trees. She'd forgotten Sandoval had no wagon.

"Go around the backside of this clump of trees," she directed. "Make sure the buckboard's out of sight. Unhitch the mules and bring them up to this cave entrance. Leave them in harness."

A couple of minutes later, Sam tethered the mules to a tree at the cavern entrance.

"Well, this is really a snug little place," he marveled, stepping inside Sandoval's former home.

She lighted the lantern she'd found and its yellow glow softened the hard look of the bare walls. "I'm guessing we have at least an hour before that storm hits, or those riders can be close enough to smell our smoke," she assumed command. "Let's make a fire and cook up a hot meal while we have a chance."

Sam worked as if he realized their situation and had a fire

47

blazing within five minutes on the flat, rocky hearth by the entrance. Lucy went to the wagon for beans, bacon, frying pan, coffee pot and a loaf of brown bread.

Little was said as they cooked and ate their meal. The afternoon light outside began to fade.

When they finished, she led Sam back into the tunnel that dead-ended into the vertical mineshaft where fresh water was only a few feet below. They let down their bucket on a rope and drew up enough water to refill their canteens and the several wooden water kegs they'd brought for the mules.

Sam seemed relieved. "Why didn't you tell me we had no water worries?"

"You never asked." She thought of the lean, dark man who'd revealed this source of pure water in the flooded mine. *Wherever you are, Carlos Sandoval, I wish you well.* Without him, neither she nor Charvein would still be alive.

"What time is it?" she asked.

Sam dug out his watch. "Five-twenty."

"I'm going to slip out and have another look."

He nodded.

Back in the cavern, she hung the binoculars around her neck and catfooted outside into the trees and crept around the base of the hill, eyes and ears attuned to anything. The gusting wind was rattling a loose shutter on one of the empty buildings. She paused just behind an old storage shed, stretched out prone and slowly put her head around the corner. The wind kicked dust into her face, and she blinked, eyes watering. When she could see again, she pulled up the binoculars and adjusted the focus. At first she saw nothing but the vacant street with whirlwinds of dust and a sign swinging on one rusty hook in front of a milliner's shop.

She jerked back. Three horsemen came around the bend at the far end of the street. Her heart began to race. She ventured another look. Their hats were pulled low and bandannas protected the lower halves of their faces. She had to remind herself they weren't as close as they appeared in the twin lenses.

The riders had outdistanced the leading edge of the brown dust cloud that was rolling out front of the advancing rain. They never hesitated, trotting their mounts and two led mules along the street. As she expected, they reined up at the rocky ruin of San Juan Church.

One of the men jerked down the bandanna and said something to the others, pointing at the pile of rock. With the glasses, Lucy saw the thin mustache and the pointed eyebrows of Ezra Pitney. She'd been right to be quick and cautious.

One of the riders dismounted and pulled two short-handled shovels from one of the mule packs. Pitney began climbing over the rock pile.

Lucy slid back, got to her feet and sprinted toward the cavern entrance in the trees.

Darting into the cave, she stopped dead at the sight of a black gun muzzle leveled at her.

"Don't surprise me like that, gal," Stonehouse holstered his Colt.

"They're here . . . Pitney and two men." She panted. "We're downwind of them, so put the feedbags on the mules before they get a scent of those animals and make a noise."

Sam could move quickly when he chose and she was glad he didn't question her authority to order him around. She'd noticed professional gamblers rarely allowed pride or emotion to interfere with practicality.

He scooped a few handfuls of grain into the nosebags and buckled them on before Lucy could even catch her breath. He brought the mules just inside the entrance while she smothered the remains of their cooking fire.

"Are they armed?" he asked.

Lucy ground her teeth. "I forgot to notice, but I'm sure they are."

"You know this Ezra Pitney?"

"Not personally. Only by sight and reputation. I hear he's a very hard man when it comes to money—especially his."

"What will they do when they discover the gold is gone?"

Lucy had been wondering the same thing. "It might take them a while to figure that out," she answered. "It's getting dark. With the wind blowing in the dust and rain pretty quick, maybe they won't notice someone's been digging there." She hoped she sounded confident, but wasn't at all sure. "We should've shoved a few rocks back in the hole to cover the remains of the altar." She couldn't think of everything.

She regretted not staying long enough on her spying jaunt just now to get a glimpse of what the other two men looked like. They appeared to be lean and muscular—just the type Pitney would pick to retrieve his gold. And they had to be trustworthy and loyal as well—and well paid—or they could easily overwhelm Pitney and take whatever they found. "Trustworthy" and "loyal" were two words that were rapidly losing their meaning for her. She had graduated into the hard world of reality, or perhaps descended into the dog-eat-dog world she saw all around her in Virginia City. She'd come to take her share of the treasure, but wasn't safely away with it yet.

While Sam washed their tin plates and utensils in a bucket of cold water, Lucy stepped out the door of the cavern. "I'll be right back."

"Don't let them spot you," Sam warned in a low voice.

"Don't worry."

She crept out of the trees and around the base of the hill. The buckskin jacket effectively hid her white blouse, and no other light-colored clothing was exposed. She pulled her hat down over her wind-tanned face.

Movement a block away. She looked through the binoculars. All three men were digging furiously in the pile of church ruins. They had reason to hurry, she thought, lowering the glasses and squinting into the gusting wind. The dust being whipped into a rolling cloud ahead of the approaching storm had reached the far end of the main street. The sun had long since disappeared and the sky was darkening with the quick-moving blackness of sudden night. The greenish-black cloud spoke of hail.

In the few seconds she looked and pondered, a blast of wind enveloped her. She ducked away from its ferocity, and trotted back toward the cavern. Before she reached it, the wind turned suddenly chill and hailstones began to clatter down all around her, bouncing off her hat brim.

"We have to go—now!" she dashed into the shelter of the cave.

"Why? This is the best place to ride out the storm."

"Rain behind this hail is probably already starting to spread out and fill those playas," she said. "We can't be stuck here with those three men."

He apparently realized the truth of her words. "I'll hitch up the team." He darted from the cavern with a sack of their eating utensils.

Sam was back in a flash and she helped him lead the mules to the buckboard and held them while he hitched them up. She had trouble controlling them; they were jumping sideways, flipping their long ears at the pelting hailstones.

"Ready!" Sam grabbed the reins to hold the team in check while Lucy unbuckled and slid off the nosebags, tossing them into the wagon. They were downwind of Lodestar and any braying would not be heard above the roar of the thunderstorm and the hailstones clattering off empty wooden buildings.

A flash of lightning lit up the scene, showing the animals walling their eyes and tossing their heads. Lucy sprang for the seat on the buckboard. She pointed south, and Sam turned the mules loose in that direction. With energy born of fear, the animals lunged ahead and Lucy was nearly thrown over the back of the seat into the wagon bed. Clutching desperately to keep her seat, she saw they still had the low ridge of hill between them and the town. Pitney and his men were probably scrambling for cover. If she and Sam could drive the team and wagon a mile away while the storm was at its worst, they wouldn't be detected.

Intermittent ridges of low desert mountains ran northwest to southeast in this region. During the frequent flashes of lightning, she could see the nearest one ahead of them, but couldn't judge its distance. If they could make it that far, they'd be safe. They had water, food and some grain. The rocky slopes and declivities would hide them. Best of all, they had the gold and would be out of sight of Pitney and his men. She felt sure they hadn't yet been seen or heard. It must remain that way if they didn't want to be tracked down and possibly shot.

While this ran through her mind, she was gripping the edge of the seat, flexing her knees when the unsprung buckboard banged and bounced, hitting ruts and gullies, slewing side to side in the wet sand. The hail had given way to a heavy downpour, slashing across the dry lakebed. The rain would wash away any tracks they made, but it might do something else. From under her bent hat brim, she squinted ahead in the flashes of lightning. The normally dun-colored surface of the playa was turning dark, with water rapidly flowing into the broad, shallow depression. If they couldn't get across before it saturated the crusty surface, the playa could become a boggy morass. They'd become flies fatally mired in mud.

The terrified mules plunged ahead in a wild attempt to escape the violence of the storm. Lucy hung on and willed the distant mountains to come rapidly closer. It was all she could do.

CHAPTER 7

Ezra Pitney swore softly to himself, clumping back and forth in the lantern light of the empty Lodestar mercantile. He paused by the broken front window and stared out at the rain slashing down. Wind was wrenching at the sagging roof of the front porch as if to tear it off. He pulled a blanket tighter around his shoulders and shivered in his wet clothes. "Damn this weather," he muttered, brushing back the wet hair plastered across his forehead. *This place would scorch a lizard eleven months of the year, and now it's freezing and hailing.*

He kept his back to the two men, Tom "Stripe" Morgan, his personal bodyguard, and Derrick McGinty, a foreman in the Overstrike mine. They were busy rummaging through the saddle packs for something to eat. Pitney didn't want his men to see how angry and frustrated he was. They might get the impression he wasn't in total control of himself or the situation.

Where was the gold? The overriding question shouted inside his head. They'd ridden all this distance only to be stopped by the weather. He and his men had been able to dig in the ruin only a short time before dust, darkness and the blustery downpour had driven them to shelter. What luck!

But, from what he'd seen in their short foray, he got the distinct impression someone had been at the ruins before him. Who? How long before? He could think of several possibilities. Perhaps Sandoval, the desert rat Charvein mentioned, had absconded with the gold. Or, Charvein lied about the gold being here at all, just to collect his pay. A third possibility was that Charvein took the treasure himself and squirreled it away before showing up at the mansion with his hand out. Two of the three scenarios involved Marc Charvein, the man he'd hired to find his stolen ingots and report the location. If there was anything worse than being robbed, it was being made a fool of. And Pitney decided Charvein had made a fool of him. Charvein had complained of not being paid enough for his efforts and said he'd never go through all the danger and discomfort again for the paltry sum of $240.

As a self-made mine owner who'd come up the hard way, Pitney considered himself a good judge of men. He'd pegged Charvein as a man of his word—someone who doggedly did his duty, no matter what. The former railroad detective certainly didn't strike him as sneaky and devious. Yet, tomorrow, when the storm passed, if they didn't find any trace of the gold in the ruins of the church, he'd be forced to conclude Charvein had never found it, had taken it for himself, or at least knew where it was.

"Hey, boss, you want some beans?" McGinty asked.

Pitney turned toward them, once more composed and in control.

"You'll have to eat 'em outa the can," McGinty said. "Can't cook nothing we brought. No grate or stove in this building. If we build a fire in here, this place'll go up like a match."

"Cold beans, huh?" Pitney reached for the spoon and the can. "Better than nothing." He forced a smile.

"Boss, if there's anything in this pile o' rock, it's damn well hid," the big, muscular Morgan said the next morning, straightening up and flexing his back. In spite of the cooler air, all three men were sweating from two hours of moving rocks and splintered wood, hacking with picks and shoveling up plaster.

"You reckon if this place was dynamited, the blast mighta blown the gold into little pieces?"

"No chance," the bigger, dark-haired Tom "Stripe" Morgan said. His nickname was a reference to an obvious phenomenon. Nature had given him a two-inch-wide strip of white hair running front to back through his dark hair. He wiped his nose with a blue bandanna. "You and I been in the mines enough to know heavy metal won't do that. Besides, the gold was in pure, smelted ingots. Too dense to blow apart."

The two men looked to Pitney for further direction.

"Take a rest break and we'll have a meal," Pitney said. Instinct told him the gold wasn't here. But he didn't confide his suspicions. "Might as well keep at this until we find it or we're sure it's not here." He swept an arm at the outlying area. "See those lakes on three sides of this town? We won't be going anywhere until those flooded playas dry up enough to support us and the horses."

McGinty and Morgan glanced at each other. "Boss, that might take a week or two," the smaller McGinty said. "Those things turn mighty swampy before the water sinks just below the surface. And we could still get mired down."

Pitney nodded. He knew McGinty was right. "In a day or two, we'll try leaving by the east end of town. Looks to be higher ground. We may have to ride back to Virginia City by a long, roundabout way."

CHAPTER 8

Lucy clung to the buckboard seat and watched in helpless wonder while Sam Stonehouse took charge and showed he could drive a span of mules as adeptly as he could palm an ace off the bottom of a deck.

Frequent lightning illuminated the rapidly flooding playa. He seemed to will the animals across, ignoring muddy spray being flung back by their flying hooves.

Before they were a half-mile out, the hail stopped, but the rain increased, gusting sideways in stinging sheets.

The protective hills drew gradually closer, but the mules began to slow and Lucy doubted they'd make it the last three hundred yards. She was prepared to throw off some of their stores, or jump down and slosh alongside the wagon to lighten the load, if necessary.

But Sam turned the team at an angle to the low mountains and seemed to instinctively find the shallowest water and the firmest footing. Even so, she held her breath, expecting the animals to flounder to a stop, leaving the relatively light buckboard up to its hubs in mud and water.

Somehow, they made it. The mules stumbled on the rising bottom and labored up out of the morass onto solid ground near the base of the rocky hills. She glanced back. Lodestar was a mile distant. She was reasonably sure no one had seen them.

The lightning flashes were becoming less frequent, and the booming thunder seemed to be moving off to the southeast, although the rain still lashed them.

Stonehouse jumped down and led the team toward a defile in the flank of the dark hills. Within a few minutes they entered a cleft in the mountain wide enough to accommodate the team and wagon. Fifty yards in, the canyon bent at a slight angle. In one of the flashes of lightning, Lucy saw the split went another few hundred yards, clear through to the other side of the low mountain range. Rivulets of water were pouring down the hillsides and rushing along in a stream toward the low playa behind them, but Lucy didn't care how soaked all their supplies were. They were out of sight of Lodestar, and the flooded lake-bed protected them from any immediate pursuit.

"You think they saw us?" she cried above the roar of the pounding rain.

"No!" he yelled back, beginning to unhitch the mules. There was no place to shelter and they couldn't get any wetter than they already were. He left the mules in harness and tied off the reins to a front wheel until the worst of the storm passed.

He and Lucy crawled under the buckboard and sat on the wet ground, listening to the rain drumming on the wooden wagon bed.

Wet and uncomfortable as she was, Lucy was still happy. They'd beaten Pitney to the gold, dug it up, escaped being seen by the mine owner and his men, and made a safe getaway. Whatever might happen from here on, they'd won the first battle. While she and Sam and the animals rested and recouped tomorrow, she'd think about where to go from here. Tomorrow they could put considerable distance between themselves and Lodestar while Ezra Pitney and his men were still marooned in the ghost town.

At the moment, she felt more confident than she had in years.

CHAPTER 9

Ehrenberg, Arizona Territory
September 21, 1885

Marc Charvein's feet stumbled against the muddy bottom and he gripped the saddle horn, letting the horse pull him up the bank as they both shed streams of reddish water from the Colorado River. The current had carried them farther downstream than he anticipated. But holding onto the saddle and swimming was better than trying to ride the stout little animal across the swift stream.

There was no ferryboat here, or he wouldn't have had to soak his clothes, boots and everything in his saddlebags, he thought, as he led his horse up the slope toward the little town.

"Give ya forty dollars for that black," a voice called from the shade of an adobe stable.

Marc Charvein cringed. The first human voice he'd heard in a week, and it came from some sharp trader trying to deal him out of his horse. He ignored the insulting offer and continued leading his mount along the dusty street.

But then he paused, considering. He had to sell his horse in order to catch the riverboat to Yuma. In a village this size, there might be few buyers. Maybe he could make a deal here. He squinted under his hat brim at a beefy, red-faced man who heaved his bulk off a bench and approached. He eyed Marc's sodden clothes and boots and the wet-slick coat of the animal.

"Took a little swim, huh? Been thinking of doing that very thing m'self, it's so damn hot."

"Didn't see a ferry at the landing," Marc said.

"There ain't one. Only Indians want to cross over the Colorado here, and they use canoes." The man gestured toward Marc's horse. "Thinking to sell him?"

"I might."

"Like I said, I'd give you forty dollars. Where'd you get that old, worn California saddle? Ain't see one o' those in years."

"I can't consider giving him away for forty dollars."

The man put a hand to his thick, gray mustache and cocked his head to one side. "Okay, tell you what—throw in that old saddle and I'll make it fifty dollars."

"Sorry. That's only half what they're worth."

"Hell, mister, you know what it costs to haul grain here from downriver? I'd have to fatten him up some to resell him. And, as you'll notice, there ain't no forage hereabouts." He waved a hand at the barren, dun-colored landscape speckled with desert sage. "These ain't the green valleys of California."

Marc was irritated. "Maybe I'll just keep him," he led his mount away. *I'll give him away before I'd sell him to that bastard.*

Fifty yards farther he spotted a saloon and tied his horse in the scant shade provided by the edge of the covered porch.

The adobe walls enclosed a dim interior that provided some relief from the glaring afternoon sun. Two men were at a table playing cards and drinking beer. They didn't look up when he entered and leaned on the bar.

"Is the beer cold?"

A grin split the face of the lean Mexican bartender. "Cold as the icicles hanging from the porch roof." He drew off a pint as he spoke.

Marc buried his nose in the foam and drank off the warm contents of the mug without stopping. "Whew!" He wiped his mouth and signaled for a refill.

He took two swallows before reaching into his vest for coins to pay. "When does winter set in here?"

"Oh, in December," the bartender said, eyeing Marc's wet, clinging clothes. "Much cooler then, *señor.* The nights are even *muy frio.*"

"Not as cold as where I just came from." It was good to hold a conversation again with someone besides himself, his mount or a thieving horse wrangler.

"Where is that?"

"Virginia City."

"Ah, in the Nevada mountains. Does everyone there have much money from the mines?"

"Not everyone. Or I wouldn't be here," Marc said. Human nature, it seemed, was ever hopeful the grass was greener somewhere else. The place he'd just left was rife with shootings, mine accidents, prostitutes, suicides, stock swindles, traveling shows, floods of whiskey, all overblown by the fierce winds of "Washoe Zephyrs," and winter blizzards. "Is that riverboat lying out yonder going down to Yuma?"

"*Si.* She leaves in the morning. You can buy a ticket from the purser on the boat."

"Know anyone who'd like to buy a good horse?"

"My swamper is a Yuma Indian who also works for an army officer and his wife nearby. But they're being transferred away and he must look for other work, maybe in the mines. He has been saving up for a horse, but ee's afraid to deal with the livery in town."

"Smart lad," Marc said. "Is he around?"

"In the back. I will call heem."

A few minutes later, the three were standing by Marc's horse while the wiry teenage Indian checked the horse's teeth, hocks and ran his hands over the animal's back. Marc had removed the saddle and dumped it on the ground.

"How much?" the boy inquired.

Marc shrugged. He felt inclined to give this young man a break.

"Fifty-five dollars. I'll throw in the saddle for free."

His dark face showed no emotion. He continued to examine the horse. "I can give you fifty."

"Close enough."

The Indian dug into a side pocket and pulled out a few crumpled bills and solemnly counted out the notes. "I do not need a saddle."

"But sure to take good care of him. Feed and water him well. He has lost weight on the trip. He's a good horse and has brought me a long way in the past few weeks."

"What is he called?" the Indian inquired.

Marc shrugged. "You can name him." He detected a slight smile on the bronze features.

"You have a sheet of paper?" he asked the bartender. "All the stuff in my saddlebags is wet."

They retreated inside and Marc wrote out a bill of sale on the bar.

"He has a long Indian name," the bartender gestured at his helper, "but everyone here knows him as Diego."

Marc finished and folded the sheet of notebook paper. "Diego, keep this just in case some white man notices the brand and accuses you of horse stealing."

Three hours later, Marc leaned back against the wall of the saloon in the shade of the porch. His boots and the contents of his saddlebags were spread out beside the building to dry in the sun. His clothes had dried on him.

He guessed this barren little town on the western edge of Arizona, unprotected by trees or hills, hadn't changed much in the past twenty years—a general mercantile, two saloons, two or three buildings that appeared to be warehouses, a stable and corral, boxy houses erected for the few residents, including the small detachment of Army personnel. Their wives who came from greener, more civilized places probably looked on this place as the last stop to hell.

An assortment of Mexicans and whites lounged in front of the general store. What in the world did they do here? The bartender told him this port was a jumping-off point for goods and machinery destined for the mines, miles to the east, and for hauling ore downriver by boat where it was transferred to the recently completed Southern Pacific Railroad that crossed east to west at Yuma.

Marc had earlier decided to follow the Colorado River down to the Mexican border, then work his way eastward to avoid riding through the rugged mountains of the Mogollon Rim. He wanted to winter far enough south where the winters were mild. But summer hadn't yet loosened its grip on this part of the Territory.

He dozed in the heat and awoke some while later, more rested. The westering sun cast long shadows up the street. He pulled on his now-dry boots, heaved the saddle and saddlebags over one shoulder and started down the slope toward the river.

The sternwheeler, *Gila*, lay tugging at her mooring lines, reddish, silt-laden water sucking around the low hull. He looked at the river, thinking of his crossing earlier in the day—a hazardous one, indeed. He hadn't considered the danger until his mount reached deeper water and began to swim. As soon as the horse lost footing, Marc slid off, clinging to the saddle horn while the strong current swept them downstream. Luckily, the horse was strong and brought them safely to shore.

Now, the heat had turned his wet, itchy clothes into dry cotton, streaked with a red residue. He was dirty, unshaven and needed a haircut.

He stepped across the gangway and looked around. Where was everyone?

"May I help you, sir?"

A slim young man dressed in a white shirt emerged from the open door of a forward office.

"I need a one-way ticket to Yuma."

The purser motioned him inside. "Your name?"

Marc told him. The purser flipped open an inkpot, dipped a steel pen and filled in a cardboard ticket in a neat hand. He stamped it and exchanged it for several limp paper dollars.

"Cabin twelve on the starboard side off the saloon on the next deck up."

"What about meals?"

"Included. A bell announces mealtimes in the main saloon."

"Any place to wash up?"

He gestured with his pen. "A limited supply of fresh water in a tank on the hurricane deck—mostly for drinking and cooking. No bathing, except for dips in the river if we happened to be tied up or aground. Pitcher and bowl in the cabin." He glanced at a clock mounted on the bulkhead. "Supper in an hour."

"I hadn't expected so many passengers in a remote place like this," Marc glanced at several men and women lined up to come aboard.

The clerk didn't look up. "Oh, some of those are military families being relieved and replaced. They're heading back to San Francisco."

Marc took his ticket, picked up his saddle and moved away. Mounting the stairs, he cast an eye over those coming aboard with luggage—two bearded, rough-looking men—maybe miners—several women in long dresses, a young mother pulling along a pouty child, several men in military blue with duffels on their shoulders, servants with valises.

One lone man at the rear carried no luggage. He was dressed in a white shirt, whipcord pants and wore a gunbelt. His face was shaded by a wide-brimmed hat. The man looked up at him and their eyes locked. Marc had a flash of recognition. Where had he seen that face before? The mustache, the long nose looked familiar. The man looked quickly away and Marc dismissed the thought; he was always seeing people he thought he knew. Certain physical types just resembled one another. It wasn't unusual.

Marc reached the top of the stairs, slung the saddle over his shoulder, then crossed through the empty main saloon, looking for the inside door of cabin twelve on the starboard side.

Dumping his saddle by the bunk, he pulled and checked his Merwin Hulbert pistol to be sure it was dry and clean after its soaking in the river. He wiped the cartridges and reloaded it. From long habit, he stayed prepared for anything—especially in a strange place.

The cabin was hot and stuffy. He swung open the window with the louvered shutter. It didn't help; the slight afternoon breeze was gone.

He removed his grainy clothing, including his underwear, shook and brushed the garments. But the dried river silt refused to let go. It seemed to impregnate the cloth. He wondered if even a thorough washing with soap would take out the brownish stains.

He removed his only change of clothing from the saddlebags—underwear, canvas pants and pale yellow cotton shirt—and pulled them on.

He splashed clean water into the bowl on the nightstand and sluiced it over his face and hands, then ran fingers through his hair.

He stropped his straight razor on his boot, but the dinner bell clanged so he laid the razor down and regarded his sun-browned face in the tiny mirror. *Good enough.*

Outside in the small main saloon, individual tables had been shoved together to form one longer one, overlaid with a tablecloth. More than a dozen people were milling about, selecting places.

"You traveling alone?" a pleasant female voice asked. He turned to see a young woman at his elbow.

"Yes."

"You're welcome to sit with us." She indicated a chair next to the one a uniformed lieutenant was holding for her.

"Thank you."

The balding soldier with the thick mustache thrust out his hand. "Kirby Selinger," he said. "This is my wife, Hope."

"Ma'am." Marc inclined his head and gripped the lieutenant's hand. "Marc Charvein."

Amid a cacophony of scraping chairs and conversations, the rest of the passengers found places at table.

Most of these people knew each other and appeared to be military officers clad in shirtsleeves in deference to the weather. He guessed all the women here were married. One young woman had a babe in her arms. There were a few other men who appeared to be laborers or miners of some kind.

A Chinese steward appeared and set two bowls of steaming meat and gravy on the table.

"Oh, Sammy Lu!" Hope Selinger exclaimed. "What a pleasure to see you again."

The Chinaman bowed politely, then withdrew. The young purser came in to help, bearing plates of steaming biscuits.

"This smells great!" Marc said.

"Don't let your appetite get too riled," Hope said under her breath. "That's actually salt beef with gravy. Nothing fresh here. No ice. But Sammy can do wonders under the worst conditions."

"After what I've been subsisting on, this is a feast," Marc said. "And I can believe you about the Chinaman."

Kirby Selinger passed the biscuits. "No butter, no milk or cream. If the boat had just come in from Yuma, we might have potatoes or greens, but since they're on a return run from farther upriver, just tinned stuff."

"Sammy can make the most delicious peach pies," she went on. "It's a wonder he can work around a stove in this weather. I'm sure the lard runs like water."

Sammy Lu reappeared with a large metal pot and began pouring coffee.

Marc filled his plate with meat, boiled rice and bread, gave silent thanks, and began to eat. It was a real relief to be among friendly people again—a definite improvement over talking to himself and his horse.

He glanced through the windows in the forward end of the saloon and noticed the westering sun was obscured, but saw no clouds. A haze seemed to be rising.

"Oh, no!" Hope gasped softly. "Here it comes again."

Marc looked his question at her.

The haze thickened rapidly, enveloping the boat, drifting through the open windows like a moist fog.

"What's wrong?"

Hope put her fork down with a clatter, her complexion pale.

"A hot steam comes off the river late in the afternoon," Lieutenant Selinger explained. "Floats over the whole town. Comes down on everyone like a steam bath."

Hope was wiping perspiration from her face with a napkin. Her skin had gone from pale to rosy. Everything in the room quickly grew clammy, and the women's dresses clung to their shoulders. The men who still wore coats shed them and rolled up their sleeves. Conversations faltered and most of those at the table stopped eating.

"Here, my dear, try this," Lieutenant Selinger took a flask from inside his coat and poured a dash of something into her coffee cup.

"I wish we had some milk punch," she raised the cup to her lips.

"Sherry and an egg usually brings her up to normal," her husband said.

"A steam bath wouldn't be too bad," Hope said, "if we could follow it with a cool shower. Thank God, this is the last one of these I'll have to endure."

The moist heat hadn't prostrated Marc, but he was definitely uncomfortable, sweating under his clean clothes. Any small breeze would help, but there was none in the breathless atmosphere.

"This place is as primitive as the Congo," she continued. "Can't keep a house clean when the floors are packed earth. "We've even had a strong earthquake since we've been here."

Marc was only half-listening when, out of the corner of his eye, he saw a figure enter the narrow saloon through an open forward door.

He glanced up at the latecomer and his stomach contracted. It was "Polecat" Morgan, Ezra Pitney's personal bodyguard. It was the man Marc had seen in line earlier and thought he recognized, but Morgan had been wearing a hat then. What in the world was Morgan doing here, so far from his boss? He was known in Virginia City as a doggedly loyal man who would never leave Pitney's side, unless so ordered by the wealthy mine owner.

Morgan paused, as if looking for an empty chair at the table, but Marc knew he was just making a grand entrance, hoping the women, old and young, would be gasping at the sight of his marvelous physique, handsome features and sweeping mustache. Six-feet high and 200 pounds of lithe muscle, he was made even more striking by the two-inch-wide stripe of white hair that ran from above his left eyebrow to the back of his head. The left eyebrow was also white, and the same peculiar lack of pigment had rendered the left half of his mustache a solid white—all in contrast to his dark brown hair. Known to one and all as "Stripe" Morgan, he was damned by his enemies as "Polecat" Morgan.

Marc looked down at his plate and pretended to eat, barely hearing what Hope Selinger was saying. "Polecat" had to be here for a reason. And Marc had been a lawman too long to think it was coincidence. He'd learned to trust his finely honed instincts, and instinct now told him "Polecat" had come for him.

Chapter 10

Virginia City, Nevada

". . . Marc Charvein . . ."

Carlos Sandoval stiffened and tuned his ears to a nearby conversation in the smoky, crowded saloon. He leaned away from the bar and tried to see around a fat man beside him.

The name of his friend had jumped out from amidst the hum of background noise. A slim man in an expensive suit leaned his back against the bar, holding a drink in one hand and a cigarillo in the other. He sported a narrow mustache, and his gray eyebrows titled up from two black eyes. He was talking to a man beside him who was the same height, but looked much bigger because of a muscular build.

Sandoval strained to hear, but their words were smothered by the cacophony of voices, laughter and a buzzing roulette wheel.

He tugged down his hat brim to further hide his face and glanced around. Charvein was nowhere in this room, but these two men had mentioned his name.

Sandoval, still a wanted man himself, was taking a big chance venturing out into the streets of Virginia City. Sancho Ramirez, whose house he was using as a refuge and hideout, assured him the name of Carlos Sandoval had not appeared in any of the newspaper accounts of the Lodestar shootout. The printed stories referred to him vaguely as a "hermit," an "old recluse," or a "lone prospector." But Sandoval was nevertheless anxious to re-outfit, then ride south with his mule and burro to seek out relatives in the Arizona Territory. Actually, he hadn't seen or heard from his cousins in so long, they probably thought he was dead. But it gave him a reason for traveling south. It was a starting point for the rest of his life.

He stepped away from the bar with his beer glass and surveyed the room, as if looking for someone. Then he turned back, carefully slid in beside the pair and signaled the bartender for a refill.

There was something vaguely familiar about both of these men, but recognition hung just outside his conscious mind. He leaned on the bar, sipping his beer and listening, cudgeling his long-unused memory of faces and names from his Virginia City days.

That slightly shrill, nasal voice—where had he heard it? He glanced quickly at them and then away.

Ezra Pitney. The name suddenly popped into his head. It was the cocky mine owner whose gold Sandoval had found hidden in Lodestar and subsisted on these past four years. A chill went up his back. If only Pitney knew who was standing next to him. Neither of the two wore a hat and the bigger man bore a white stripe through his dark hair, front to back, just to the left of center. This must be the notorious Stripe Morgan, or "Polecat" Morgan, Pitney's personal bodyguard Sandoval had heard about.

". . . ask around. See if you can catch any word of him," Pitney was saying. "Haven't seen him in town since he came to the house and collected his pay more than a week ago."

"What about the girl he was traveling with?" Stripe Morgan asked. "What was her name? Lucy . . . something?"

"Barkley," Pitney said. "Lucinda Barkley, the sheriff told me. Have a hunch if we find her, we'll find Charvein. Trouble is, I wouldn't know her if she walked up to me. But she might just be the hole card in this deal. The bartender at the Silver Stope told me she left town with a gambler the same night Charvein collected his pay."

"What gambler?"

"Sam Stonehouse."

"Ah, yes." Morgan nodded. "Everybody knows Sam."

The pair was silent for several seconds.

"If I can turn over a few rocks and catch Charvein's scent, you want me to follow him?" Morgan asked.

"Damn right. Go after him before he blows all my gold or gets himself killed over it. I'm sure he's probably left town. Nose around the depot ticket office, all the liveries, and stage station. Maybe you can pick up a hint of where he's gone." He sipped his whiskey. "After you and I found nothing in Lodestar, it's obvious why he was in such a hurry to disappear."

"I'll get on it first thing in the morning."

"No. Start today. The longer we wait, the farther away he'll be. I'll stay here and see if I can cut the track of the girl and the gambler. Don't know how they figure into this, but . . ."

Sandoval glanced up to see him staring vacantly at the mirror on the back bar. "While Charvein was standing in my house and I was paying him," Pitney said in a deadly monotone, "he already had the rest of my gold stashed away, ready to hightail it. I hate being made a fool of."

The mine owner seemed to be working himself into a lather, his face slightly flushed. He took another sip of whiskey.

"He knows me on sight, but don't reckon he'll be expecting me," Morgan said.

"Be careful. He'll be watching his backtrail."

"You can bet on it. But first thing I have to do is pick up his track." He smoothed the ends of his half-white mustache before tilting up his beer.

"If you lay hands on the bastard, make sure he has no fatal

accidents 'til you find out if he still has my gold, or how much
of it's been spent or stashed."

Sandoval cringed at the threat, knowing nuggets of that same
gold were in his own pocket at the moment. The rest of the gold
was missing from the church ruins? Sandoval was stunned. Had
Charvein actually returned and dug it out after promising to
leave it alone?

Sandoval had taken three ingots of gold and melted them
into insignificant-looking grainy nuggets. Just before leaving the
ghost town he'd packed the nuggets in tiny sacks on his burro,
Lupida, along with other supplies. *Ah, Providence must still be
with me,* he thought. *I rode out only two days before early autumn
rain made the dry playa an impassable lake.*

He finished his beer and slid away from the bar, head down.

"Marc Charvein?" The livery owner arched his eyebrows at
Sandoval as he weighed the grains of gold on his balance scales.
"Yeah, he was here."

Sandoval shot a glance at his barrel-chested friend, Sancho
Ramirez, who lounged against the doorframe of the office.

"You know him?" the liveryman dropped the tiny nuggets
into a money drawer and handed Sandoval his change in silver
coin.

"He's a friend of mine," Sandoval said. "I'm just passing
through and wanted to say howdy."

"He bought a horse from me and said he was leaving town
on a long trip. Don't recall where."

Sandoval and Ramirez exchanged a significant look.

"When was that?" Ramirez asked.

"Umm . . . I reckon maybe ten, twelve days ago." The liveryman led the way out of the dusty office into the stables. He
swung open the doors of adjacent stalls and brought out the
burro, Lupida, and the mule, Jeremiah, handing over their reins.

"They been groomed and rested and grain fed. Nice animals."

Lupida nuzzled Sandoval. "No treats yet," he rubbed her nose. He led them out into the sunshine where he looped the reins around a wheel rim of his friend's wagon. Ramirez swung a saddle blanket over Jeremiah's back, patted it into place and followed with a double-rigged saddle.

The livery owner came to the door to watch. "Ya know, you're the second person today looking for Charvein."

"Yeah?" Sandoval said, his back to the man. "Who else?" He feigned indifference.

"Big guy. White stripe in his hair. Think he works at the Over-strike mine."

"Oh. Well, maybe I'll run into Marc next trip." He shrugged and continued to adjust the packsaddle on the burro. "You sure he didn't mention where he was bound on his trip?"

The liveryman shook his head. "I got a pretty good memory, but I don't believe he said, and I had no reason to ask."

"Thanks for taking good care of my animals." He thrust out his hand and they shook.

"Come back any time."

Sandoval mounted his mule and took up the long lead of the burro trailing behind with the loaded packsaddle.

Ramirez climbed into his wagon and clucked to the team. He followed Sandoval along the crowded Virginia City street. They rode to the south end of town and continued along the road into the adjacent town of Gold Hill where they pulled up. Sandoval edged his mule closer to the wagon and the two gripped hands.

"Keep my bunk made up," Sandoval said. "I might be back sooner than you think."

"May the Virgin of Guadalupe bring you back without harm."

"She's had her hands full up to now."

Ramirez grinned. "Wire me at Wells Fargo. You're welcome to

stay here as long as you like. *Mi casa es su casa.*"

"*Gracias,* but I've been a burden to you and your wife enough for now. Houseguests don't wear well after a week. *Adios, mi amigo.*" He bowed, then urged Jeremiah forward toward whatever awaited him down south.

CHAPTER 11

Charvein lost his appetite and knew it wasn't due to the suffocating fog enveloping the boat.

"Polecat" Morgan had taken a seat several feet away on the opposite side of the table and was filling his plate, exchanging pleasantries with a man on his right.

Charvein nodded at the remarks of Hope Selinger as she sipped her brandy-laced coffee and complained of the enervating weather.

Why did the presence of this man from Virginia City fill him with sudden dread? He couldn't explain it. He tried to shake off the feeling and concentrate on his food. It would seem very odd if he suddenly left the table. He ate slowly, chewing each mouthful thoroughly and forcing himself to swallow, although his stomach was in knots. Should he acknowledge this man as he would an old acquaintance? Charvein thought they might have been introduced at some time, but couldn't quite recall.

Slowly he began to relax, and his appetite returned. Logically, there was no reason to be nervous. He ate all he could comfortably hold and pushed his plate away. He pretended to listen with interest to Hope Selinger, and even asked her a few questions about the town of Ehrenberg. Twenty minutes later the heated fog began to lift and disperse and the remainder of the company at the table was recovering from its effects as normal conversation resumed.

The Chinese cook appeared with three peach pies sliced into

wedges and set them on the table.

Although the dessert had a delicious aroma, Charvein passed on any more to eat. His stomach had been accustomed to scant rations so long, he didn't want to push it.

Hope talked to him exclusively now, and Charvein noticed Lieutenant Selinger, seated on her far side, was engrossed in a lively conversation about politics with a man on his left.

"Marc, forgive me for asking such a personal question, but are you married by any chance?" Hope asked in an undertone, looking sideways at him.

Caught off guard, he answered honestly, "No. So far, I've remained a bachelor." Uncomfortable, he tried to make light of it. "Afraid I'm not a very good prospect."

"I haven't known you long, but I'd judge that's probably not the case at all," she said with a sly, coquettish smile. "I'd guess you probably have a well-concealed wild streak about you that just drives girls mad with desire." She continued to eat as if she'd said nothing out of the ordinary.

His heartbeat picked up slightly. Did she always talk to strange men this way? He glanced at her husband who was pushing some argument to his friend and looking the other way. He swallowed and continued to joke about it. "Why yes, ma'am, as a matter of fact, you've found me out. I'm a regular Don Juan."

"I thought as much," she said in a serious tone. "A man with your looks and charm . . ." She left the sentence unfinished.

She dropped her napkin into her lap and as she retrieved it, her hand seemed to briefly caress his thigh.

Now he was in a quandary. How should he react to this? What was she up to? Her husband was sitting close by. On a quick impulse, he turned the conversation in another direction. "Do you and the lieutenant have any children?"

"No." She seemed surprised by the question. "But Kirby has

a ten-year-old son by his first wife. She died in childbirth at some outpost in Wyoming. I'm considerably younger than he is, you know," she added.

Charvein would have guessed this, but she seemed to emphasize the point. Maybe she was a bored Army wife, being dragged from post to post, withering on the vine, no social contacts except with other bored wives and no children to occupy her time and energy. He couldn't imagine why Kirby wasn't keeping a good-looking young wife like this amorously satisfied. Maybe flirting with strangers was her sole adventure in life. Perhaps she was all talk and would panic at any actual advances her flirting might attract.

Whatever the situation, he was very uneasy, and suddenly had a thought that might deflect this personal conversation. "Don't look now, but that man with the white streak in his hair across the way . . ."

"Yes," she said, her long lashes screening a glance over the rim of her coffee cup. Charvein could smell the brandy.

"I met him once in Virginia City. It would be a great service to me if you could find out what he's doing on this boat and where he's bound."

She cut a piece of pie and didn't respond immediately.

"His name is Stripe Morgan," Charvein went on under his breath. "He used to be the personal bodyguard of a mine owner named Ezra Pitney."

"I don't think this boat stops before we get to Yuma," she said quietly. "That's where he has to be going, unless, of course, he's headed on down to the gulf to catch a ship."

"I have a hunch his presence here has something to do with me."

She pursed her full lips, her fair complexion still flushed, whether from the heat or sudden excitement of this clandestine assignment, he couldn't tell.

"You'll fill me in on the details later?" She arched her brows at him.

"Of course."

"When?"

He took a deep breath. He couldn't lay out his whole past to this woman he'd just met. But if she could find out about Stripe . . . maybe he'd tell her some of his story. He wiped his mouth and spoke behind the napkin. "I'll be on the hurricane deck about sundown in an hour or so." He pushed back from the table and rose, feeling the boat vibrate as the steam engine swung the vessel into the current.

CHAPTER 12

Hope did not appear on the hurricane deck that evening. Her husband, Lieutenant Kirby Selinger, did come up with a group of other men. They lounged by the rail, smoking cigars and talking.

Several women came topside to stroll around and enjoy the slight breeze caused by the motion of the *Gila* plowing downstream. It was by no means cool yet, and the red-gold sunset that spread across the western sky gave no hint of any coming weather change.

A half-dozen children ran and chased each other around the deck, yelling, their shrill voices almost welcome to Charvein's ears after so many days of silence on his lonely ride south.

Leaning both elbows on the starboard rail, he stood by himself and stared at the glorious sunset, wondering if he'd been wise to even mention Stripe Morgan to Hope Selinger. How trustworthy was she? How discreet? Stripe was also nowhere to be seen, and Charvein began to think maybe Hope was working her feminine wiles on the big man.

The sunset finally flamed out in a welter of red and gold. Purple dusk slid away to night. Charvein waited another hour, abandoning expectations of Hope showing up. A gibbous moon was silvering the river and the desert on either side, so apparently the captain had decided to continue on as long as visibility was good, instead of tying up for the night.

Charvein breathed deeply of the clean desert air—a peaceful

night. Shortly, some of the passengers began to drag their bedding up onto the open deck and spread it out. Apparently this was more tolerable than the stuffy cabins below. Men and women both wore the smallest amount of loose, thin clothing that they could get by with. Informality among long-time friends.

He finally went below to the next deck and approached his cabin from the outside, along the catwalk. Just as he reached for his key, the boat heeled a fraction and the door swung outward a few inches. He stopped still, a chill going up his back. He let go of the key and instead gripped the butt of his pistol, his pulse quickening. He strained to hear anything above the soft throbbing of the steam engine below and the quiet voices above on the next deck. Nothing.

He took a cautious step forward and put his hand on the door handle, sliding the tips of his fingers below to the keyhole. He felt splinters and bent metal where the lock had been pried loose. No light came from his room. He waited another thirty seconds. Silence. Drawing the pistol, he muffled it under his vest to draw the hammer to full cock. Then he gripped the edge of the door, flung it open and leapt inside and away from the opening, sweeping the dark room with the gun.

Faint light from outside showed the room was empty.

Still holding his gun at the ready, he went to the table, fumbled for a match and lit the lamp in the wall sconce. The few possessions from his saddlebags were strewn on the floor. Someone had slashed the mattress of his bunk, and the stuffing was scattered about.

There came a soft rap on the inside door. He started, then moved next to the wall, holding his gun steady. "Who is it?"

"It's Hope."

Still gripping his pistol, he slid back the bolt and opened the door. Even in the uncertain light of the lamps inside the saloon, her face was white. He pushed open the door far enough for her to slip inside. What if her husband came looking for her at that moment?

She glanced at the room and then at his gun. "So he *was* here."

"You mean Stripe Morgan?" He shoved the gun into the holster under his vest.

"Yes." She sat down on the edge of his bunk. "He had his hand wrapped in a handkerchief, and I saw some blood . . ."

Charvein went to the outside door with the broken latch and struck a match. There was a trace of blood on a sharp piece of bent metal, and three drops on the door sill. He pulled the door to. "You talked to him?"

"Yes," she said quietly. "Actually, I was very friendly, but apparently he'd already been up here and wasn't inclined to talk. Very distracted."

"He gave no hint about this?" He gestured at the mess.

"Well, he seemed very angry and upset about something."

"Whatever he was after, he apparently didn't find it. I don't have much with me—surely nothing worth stealing. The only money I have is in my pocket. But I haven't had time to look around to see if anything's missing."

They were silent for a few moments.

"Are you going to tell me what's going on?" she asked in a slightly unsteady voice.

"I wish I knew. I told you I'd known him only casually in Virginia City. He was the personal bodyguard for a mine owner there—a man named Ezra Pitney. Pitney hired me to track an ex-convict who'd stolen and hidden some of Pitney's gold. But I never had any connection with this Stripe Morgan. Don't think I ever met the man—just knew him by sight and reputation."

"Maybe Mr. Pitney sent his bodyguard to follow you for

some reason," she suggested. The lamplight showed her complexion regaining a little of its color.

"I don't know. Did Morgan say where he was headed?"

"No. But after a few minutes he began to warm up to me and suggested I might visit his cabin and have a drink. Before I could even make an excuse, Kirby came along and said he was taking our bedding topside to sleep in the open air with the others."

"You'd better go on, then, before the lieutenant begins to suspect something with you in here."

She rose and put her hand on the door handle.

"Did you see which cabin Morgan is in?"

"Don't know the number, but it's the one far aft on this same starboard side."

"Thanks, Hope. You've been a great help."

She smiled and glided close to him. "Maybe you can tell me more details of the story about your adventures of working for that mine owner."

"Tomorrow, perhaps, after I clean this place up and get some sleep," he stalled. She seemed entirely too friendly. Or was she always this way with strange men? How much did Kirby Selinger know about this attractive wife of his?

She opened the inside door a crack and peeked out. Charvein could see over her shoulder the main saloon was deserted.

She slid out, turned and gave him a long look, then closed the door softly after her.

Charvein cleared up the cabin, even stuffing the padding back into the torn mattress. When he finished, it was nearly eleven o'clock. He sat down on the edge of the bunk, planning his next move. Thanks to Hope, he was almost certain who'd broken in. Nothing seemed to be missing, so Morgan hadn't found whatever he was searching for.

What should he do now? He felt sure the burglar wouldn't be

back since the place had apparently been thoroughly ransacked and the thief knew Charvein was now on the alert.

He'd confront the big man in the morning. Right now, he was exhausted and had to have some sleep. Even though he couldn't lock the broken door, he felt relatively safe. Just to be sure, he dragged the mattress off the bunk and put it next to the inside door where he'd be alerted if anyone tried to enter. The nightstand would shield him from the outside door. He turned down the lamp, leaving only a low, soft light, then lay down with his boots on, sliding the loaded pistol under the saddle that served as a pillow.

But, tired as he was, he was too keyed up to sleep. He lay on his back staring up at the ceiling and thinking. Surely, even Pitney, who was fiercely protective of his property, wouldn't go to the extreme of sending his man to take back the unspent portion of the $240 in gold that Charvein had honestly earned. It made no sense. There must be some other reason for Morgan to be here. Perhaps Morgan had quit his job or been fired and was now freelancing, desperate for money. But there were a lot more inviting targets right there in Virginia City—unless Morgan thought Charvein had left town with a lot more gold.

What kind of man was Morgan? He was reputed to be doggedly faithful to his boss. Charvein couldn't puzzle it out. There was no point in even speculating. He closed his eyes and tried to relax. But, a half-hour later, he was still awake. He had to end this uncertainty tonight. He got up and turned up the lamp to check his Merwin Hulbert, replacing the six-inch barrel with the four-inch one for close work, hoping he wouldn't have to use it.

Then he turned down the wick and went out the door into the deserted main saloon and along the carpeted floor to the room Hope had identified. No light showed beneath the door. He put his ear to the wooden panel. No sounds of breathing or snoring. Stepping softly away, he made a thorough tour of the three decks of the steamer. The only passengers still up were a young couple strolling in the moonlight on the hurricane deck. Dark, huddled forms showed where the others were sleeping in the open air.

Below, on the main deck, a crewman was on duty stoking the glowing coals through an open fire door, his face sweating in the glare of light. Two other crewmen were lounging on a pile of cordwood, smoking and talking. Moonlight silvered the water sliding alongside the boat. He walked aft to where the long pistons stroked smoothly and water frothed white, swishing from beneath the paddlewheel.

He looked carefully into all the darkened corners on each deck. But, except for the helmsman in the pilothouse, no one else was about.

He went back to Morgan's cabin from inside the darkened main saloon. Gripping the door handle, he gently pressed it down. To his surprise, it wasn't locked. He drew his revolver with his left hand and softly pushed the door open.

Someone clamped his right arm and flung him across the room. He fell against the bunk, but rolled away just before a big form landed on him. Fingers clutched his shirt in the dark and he jerked back, ripping off the buttons, but his left wrist hit the bedpost and the gun went spinning away to skitter across the floor. He sprang to a crouch, facing the assailant he could barely make out by tiny slits of moonlight slanting through the louvered window.

Suddenly a lamp flared up and the inside cabin door slammed. Charvein saw Morgan five feet away, ready to spring. He tensed for the attack.

But then Morgan straightened up, smiling, and glanced toward the door. Charvein followed his gaze and suddenly felt sick.

Cheeks flushed and eyes flashing, Hope Selinger stood there, holding a pocket pistol trained on him.

CHAPTER 13

The bottom fell out of Charvein's stomach. But fear of an even further humiliation forced him to quell the sudden nauseous feeling. He was sure he already looked like the biggest fool in captivity. How easily he'd fallen into this trap!

"What's this?" His own voice sounded like some stranger's.

"Have a seat." Morgan gestured at the only chair in the tiny room. He made no move to draw his own weapon.

Charvein moved on weak knees and sat down. He looked from one to the other of his captors. How did Hope fit into this? Out of the corner of his eye, he caught the glint of his nickel-plated Merwin Hulbert where it'd slid under the bunk.

Morgan put a foot on the edge of the bunk and rested a forearm on his knee. "Keep him covered in case he takes a notion to try something stupid," the big man said. He stared at Charvein. "I'll get right to the point. Before you leave this cabin, you'll tell me what you've done with Mr. Pitney's gold you stole from Lodestar."

"What?" Charvein was stunned. "You . . . Pitney . . . actually think I took that?" He stalled while his mind tried to catch up to this sudden development. The accusation had taken him completely by surprise. He was sure his incredulity registered in his face.

"You're wasting time. Just give me a simple answer."

"When I collected my pay from Pitney, I told him exactly where to find his remaining gold." He glanced at Hope, wonder-

86

ing. How much did she know? Had she fallen under the spell of this handsome man and switched sides? Where was her husband?

"And where was that, *exactly*?" Morgan demanded.

"In the ruins of the church at Lodestar."

"It's not there and you know it."

"I saw a few ingots and the bell clappers in the church and nobody moved them before the building was dynamited and collapsed."

"Oh, so you blasted the church; it didn't just burn down? I was wondering how that stone building was so completely destroyed, yet big slabs of roof weren't even scorched.

"You went there?"

"Mr. Pitney and I and another fella spent three days blistering our hands combing through those ruins. There was no trace of gold." His lips set in a grim line and his jaw muscles corded.

"That gold must have weighed a good hundred pounds or more. You think I'm lugging that load of metal around with me?"

"Then you stashed it somewhere. You were the last one to see it."

Charvein drew a deep breath. Had Carlos Sandoval broken his promise not to touch the buried treasure? Charvein couldn't believe it. But what other explanation could there be? Sandoval was in the ghost town after everyone else had left. He'd been the sole custodian of that bullion for four years; he must have had a change of heart and decided to keep it all. If that's what'd happened, Charvein was not about to betray his friend. In any case, Stripe Morgan would think Carlos Sandoval was some imaginary figure Charvein had dreamed up to blame and to save himself. Morgan would never believe the little hermit even existed.

"So Pitney sent you after me? Well, he's mistaken." Charvein gave a dismissive shrug as if it was just a big mistake. "I told him the truth."

"Then how do you explain the missing gold?"

"Honestly, I can't."

"You'll have to do better than that. An innocent man doesn't run."

"I'm not running."

"You lived in Virginia City for years. Why'd you suddenly take off right after this happened?"

"I had no job and wanted to spend the winter in a warmer climate. Start fresh."

Morgan took his foot off the bunk and pulled himself up to his full height. "Frankly, Charvein, I thought you had more imagination than that. You can come up with a better story—something more convincing."

"The truth isn't always dramatic." Charvein almost added, "you arrogant bastard," but stopped himself just in time. He was in no position to irritate this man. Frustrated, he glared at the woman. "Hope, what the hell are you doing? Why're you involved in this?"

"My stage name is Claudine Amore," she said.

"The best actress to ever grace the theaters of the West," Morgan added with obvious pride.

"What about Kirby Selinger?"

"He's not my husband—just a member of our troupe of players."

"Not a bored Army wife," Charvein muttered. Never had he felt so foolish and helpless.

"I was told you were a lawman." She laughed softly.

The sarcasm burned into his soul. "I used to be." A niggling doubt played at the edges of his mind. Then it came to him. "Why the elaborate ruse?" Charvein challenged Morgan with a look. "You scared to come against me, straight up?"

"I'm a man who doesn't take chances," Morgan said. "You

were rumored to be fast with a gun after that fight in Lodestar. And I didn't know what kind of precautions you were taking to cover your backtrail. Didn't want to be dry-gulched." He nodded at Claudine. "A beautiful woman is always a distraction to throw a man off his guard. So, before I left Virginia City, I hired these two who'd just finished a week-long run of *MacBeth*. They had no immediate engagements."

"How'd you know where I was?"

"Got a line on you from the gunsmith who mentioned you were headed for the Arizona Territory. Claudine, Kirby and I caught the train to San Francisco, then down the coast to Los Angeles where the Southern Pacific brought us east to Yuma. Since nobody'd seen you there, we took the *Gila* north to the headwaters of the Colorado, figuring you'd follow the river instead of the rugged interior. And just as we were coming back south, who should we run into but a fleeing thief named Marc Charvein." He grinned at his own cleverness. "It's easier to hide in a crowded city than out here in the wide open spaces where every stranger is noticed."

"All this seems rather expensive."

"Mr. Pitney can afford it."

"But is it really worth it?"

"He thinks so. It's the principle of the thing."

"Yeah, I forgot. He'll track a man across an ocean or a desert for a silver three-cent piece." This whole situation had the unreality of a bad dream. He hoped he'd wake up soon.

"Well, now that you know what I'm after, you might as well tell me what you've done with it, and save yourself a lot of time and grief."

"This is some crazy game," Charvein said. "Even if I *had* taken it, I could tell you I spent it all—maybe bought a mansion in California or something, and what could you do about it?"

"If I was convinced of that, I'd shoot you and dump your

body in the river," Morgan said as calmly as if commenting on the weather.

"Just based on the suspicion that I stole your boss's gold?"

"Not suspicion—*certainty*. Nobody steals from Ezra Pitney and gets away with it." A tight smile stretched the sweeping mustache. "If your body washed up somewhere downstream with a hole in your head, they'd think you committed suicide or were gunned down by some bandit. The boss says he doesn't think you have any kin to come asking questions."

The sobering reality of his predicament began to settle in. Morgan was right. Charvein realized he was on his own and could expect no outside help. Even Lucinda Barkley would never know. If Morgan, after the murder, removed all identification from his victim's pockets, whoever found the body would just shovel it under the sandy soil along the river, and he'd be forgotten like hundreds of others in this remote wilderness. Maybe on a slow news day a brief notice would appear in some small-town newspaper that the body of an unknown man was found in the river. More likely, the swirling Colorado currents would bury his bones beneath a sandbar and no one would ever know what happened to him. But at that point, he wouldn't care. Anonymity was eventually the fate of everyone.

He drew a deep breath as if trying to hang onto the life that was perilously close to slipping away. He wasn't dead yet and his confidence was returning. He'd call this man's bluff. "I'll tell you one more time that I had nothing to do with stealing Pitney's gold. I have only what's left of the $240 he paid me to find out where his bullion was stashed. That's as plain as I can state it. This is all a big mistake." He stretched his arms wide and yawned. "Now, I'm going to leave, go to my cabin and get some sleep." He stood up and pointed at Morgan. "I see you have a fresh cut on your left hand. In the morning, if I feel like hassling you, I'll report to the captain you broke into my cabin and ransacked it. I found blood on the sharp metal of my door latch."

"If he tries to leave, shoot him," Morgan said to Claudine.

She frowned at him. "I'm your hired help, not your executioner," she snapped.

Morgan pulled his own six-gun. "Then I'll do it."

"Two reasons you won't," Charvein's heart pounded as he turned toward the door. "First of all, the sound of the shot would bring people running and the first mate would arrest you for murder. And second, you'd never find the gold I stashed, and Pitney would then suspect you of taking it for yourself."

"Ah, so you *did* take it,"

As Charvein stepped toward Claudine, he heard the double-click of Morgan's single-action being cocked behind him, and the big man said, "I could always say I shot an intruder who tried to rob me at gunpoint." His voice sounded strangely high-pitched.

Oh God, my bluff didn't work, Charvein thought. *And my .32 is still under the bunk.* There was no way he could reach it without taking a bullet from Morgan. "I wouldn't want to be in your shoes when you tell Pitney you killed me without finding his gold," he said over his shoulder.

He put his hand to the door handle and spoke to Claudine, "As for you . . ." He never finished the sentence. In a blur of blue material, her leg came up and a sharp kick in the groin from a pointed shoe brought him, gasping, to his knees. A second later, the heavy weight of Stripe Morgan landed on his back, slamming him to the floor.

Through the nauseating pain radiating up into his lower abdomen, Charvein heard a voice close to his head. "Good work, Claudine. I always suspected you were as deadly as a female scorpion."

The kick totally disabled him for the time it took Morgan to drag him across the room and secure his hands behind him to the bedpost, using a torn strip of wool blanket.

Morgan stood up, panting, a wild gleam in is eyes. "Now, we'll see how steady your nerves are," he said. "We'll find out shortly if you love your life more than you love gold."

He went to the door. "Watch him for a minute." He left the room.

Before the pain in Charvein's groin subsided, Morgan was back, lugging Charvein's saddle with a coil of rope. "Mighty convenient of you to be carrying this lariat on your saddle," he dropped his load on the lower bunk. He removed the torn blanket strip from Charvein's wrists and refastened them with one of the thin rawhide ties from the saddle. He dragged the mattress off the upper berth. Then he threw a clove hitch over the saddle horn, tossed the loose rope over the frame of the upper berth and tied a slipknot in the other end to form a noose. He dropped the noose over Charvein's head, pulling it up so it just touched his throat.

A cold ball of fear settled into Charvein's stomach when he felt the rough hemp rubbing against his Adam's apple. One end of the rope was around his neck, and the rope led up and across the upper berth frame and down to the saddle horn. Morgan removed a thin rawhide tie from the saddle and tied one end to the bed frame, suspending the heavy saddle with the other end. He adjusted the slack so if the thin rawhide tie broke, the saddle would drop straight down off the end of the top bunk two feet before the rope straightened and caught it above the floor, yanking the slipknot tight around Charvein's neck.

At first Charvein didn't see what Morgan was about. But then the big man went to the wall sconce, removed the burning coal oil lamp and turned up the wick. Dragging up the chair, he sat down near the bunk and proceeded to place the yellow tip of flame just under the thin rawhide tie that supported the weight of the saddle.

Charvein watched with growing apprehension. He began to suspect Polecat Morgan was mentally tilted—a man who fashioned torture for entertainment. A demonic smile stretched Morgan's black and white mustache.

"We'll conduct a little experiment," he said. He pulled out a pocket watch and flipped open the case. "Wonder how long it'll take this flame to burn through the rawhide. Let's hope your memory improves before this rawhide thong snaps. Otherwise . . ."

He didn't need to elaborate. Charvein couldn't quite twist around enough to see the whole setup, but the look of horror in Claudine's eyes told him all he needed to know. The tether would break, and the saddle would drop about two feet, yanking the noose tight. It might not be enough to break his neck, but could crush his larynx and probably cause slow strangulation.

Morgan passed the tip of yellow flame slowly back and forth beneath the taut strap.

Her back to the wall, Claudine watched, grim-faced and silent. She produced a small silver flask and nipped at it, her gaze glued to the spectacle

In the close atmosphere, the smell of burning coal oil slowly began to mingle with the acrid odor of scorching leather.

CHAPTER 14

Charvein had to force down the thrill of fear and think calmly, quickly. Maybe he could lie his way out of this.

"If I tell you where it is, will you let me go?" He let a cringing whine creep into his voice to give this maniac the satisfaction of dominating a helpless victim. A cocky, overconfident man was usually a careless man.

"Now, you know that can't happen," Morgan said. "I can't trust you to tell me the truth. You'll have to take me to it." His tone was that of an adult explaining something to a dim-witted child.

Charvein wondered what sort of hiding place might sound logical. A hundred pounds would not have been an excessive weight for his horse to carry on a leisurely ride through the California hills—especially if he walked, leading the animal part of the time. Could he say he'd deposited it in a bank along the way? No. Too easy to disprove. Some remote canyon or cave? It didn't have to be a real place. Somewhere distant enough that it would take several days to reach—ample time and opportunities for escape.

His back was against the bedpost with his wrists tied together behind it. Morgan had pulled the tether tight, so it was chaffing his skin and numbing his hands. But knots on a dry rawhide lace couldn't be snugged up as securely as knots on a rope or a blanket strip. He began to work his hands, flexing his forearms and twisting his wrists. He could feel sweat trickling down his cheeks.

Claudine stood, flask in hand, watching Morgan tease the taut rawhide strip with the tongue of flame.

To mask his writhing, Charvein kept up a distracting monologue. "Never seen a man tortured before, Claudine?" he asked.

Where, before, she'd appeared alluring, then decisively brutal, she now seemed hesitant and nervous, licking her full lips. Her eyes darted from Morgan to Charvein.

"You better tell him what he wants to know," she finally said.

"Or what?" Charvein had to assume a bravado he didn't feel. "Did you ever see a man hang? Well, you're about to—except that I'll be sitting down when it happens and will slowly choke to death. Not a pretty sight." He continued struggling to free his hands while Morgan concentrated on placing the flame. "Better take a good look so you won't forget," Charvein stared at Claudine. "This will make a good, dramatic scene for one of your plays. Only this is real life, thanks to your friend and employer, here."

"Git on outa here, Claudine!" Morgan snapped. "He's just tryin' to play on your sympathy."

She hesitated.

"Git! I'll come get you if I need you."

She capped the silver flask and slid it into her wrist bag. With one last look, she turned the door handle and quietly departed, closing the door behind her.

Silence filled the tiny cabin.

Thirty seconds later Morgan asked, "Are you thinking about it?"

"Don't talk. I'm praying."

"What?" This statement seemed to shake Stripe Morgan. His hand holding the lamp wavered away from the thin rawhide.

"I'm preparing to die," Charvein said.

"You're willing to die for gold?" He seemed incredulous, as if not quite sure what to do next.

"If I tell the truth, I die; if I lie, I live." Charvein thought to confuse the big man whom he judged to be a dogged, straightforward type, but not a deep thinker.

"Just a minute ago, you said you'd stolen it."

"I said your boss would have your head if you killed me and didn't find out where his gold was." Charvein tried to sound as if he were reconciled to his fate.

"Better be ready to have your damned neck stretched," Morgan growled, as if grimly determined to go through with it. "This thong's about burnt through. It can't hold much longer. You aren't so tough. I can see you sweatin'." He grinned as if enjoying the spectacle. "Maybe this rope will only choke you *half* to death. Then, if you change your mind, you can write down the location of the gold if you can't talk anymore." He laughed aloud as if that mental picture was some ludicrous joke.

Charvein had been struggling to free his bound wrists since before Claudine left. Perspiration moistened his forearms and hands, making them slide easier. He held his breath with the effort, staring at Morgan to make sure he was looking away toward his task of burning the thong.

Suddenly he felt a loop of the rawhide slide over his hand, and the rest of the rawhide strip loosened and fell away behind him. Sweat was stinging his eyes. He stopped moving, hoping the big man hadn't noticed.

"Last chance!" Morgan said.

But he'd miscalculated. The rawhide thong snapped and Charvein instantly snatched at the rope above his head to catch the weight of the falling saddle. The noose yanked against his throat, but not with great force. He jerked the noose off over his head.

With a yell, Morgan dropped the brass lamp and lunged toward his freed prisoner. Their hands locked on each other's throats and they fell against the lower bunk while burning coal oil streamed across the deck toward the outside door.

Charvein knew he was in trouble. He was no match for this muscular man whose hands were finishing the work of the noose. He saw spots of light before his eyes. The circulation hadn't fully returned to Charvein's hands, and he lost his grip. In desperation, he kneed Morgan in the stomach, heaving the bigger man off. They rolled over and Morgan landed in the burning kerosene.

"Ahhh!" He sprang up. "I'm on fire!" The big man flopped down on his back on the mattress, smothering the flames.

Charvein dove under the bunk and grabbed his pistol. He scrambled out the other side, barely avoiding the flames, and struggled to his feet. Morgan came up off the mattress, his back smoking but not flaming. He reached for his holster, and Charvein fired a wild shot, missing. But it made Morgan flinch and duck, giving Charvein a few seconds to slam his bootheel into the outboard door. The thin wood splintered and his momentum carried him out onto the catwalk and into the railing. A gunshot blasted from behind him.

Charvein leapt to the top of the rail, launching himself into space, arcing out over the side of the steamer. He caught his breath, seeming to fall forever, then put his feet together, bracing for impact.

With a mighty splash he hit the river and everything went quiet as he sank down and down into the cool water. His boots barely touched bottom and he kicked to the surface, gasping, when his head popped up. The wash of the passing hull thrust him away a few feet. He could see the flames still lighting up the cabin on the second deck.

"Fire! Fire!" Morgan was shouting.

The thrashing paddlewheel kicked him out into the frothing wake and the lights of the steamer rapidly receded downstream.

He treaded water, still gripping his pistol. More shouts—the alarm spreading. Feet thudded on the decks; the crew scrambled to fight one of the deadliest enemies of any boat—fire. The paddlewheel slowed, but the steamer was already sixty yards downstream. Charvein knew the boat wasn't slowing to rescue a man overboard. Crewmen were dashing for containers of sand; some were lowering buckets and scooping water from overside.

He holstered his gun and watched the boat fade away. After a minute or so, his boots became heavy, and he kicked toward the east bank. Finally, he staggered up from the water through a clump of marshy reeds and climbed out onto the dry, moonlit desert.

He took off his shirt and wrung it out. The night air blew chilly on his wet body. He'd better move away from the river and find some kind of shelter in this mostly treeless landscape. Stripe Morgan had proved persistent so far and would likely still come after him. But Charvein was banking on the excitement of the fire to slow down or stop any immediate pursuit. Morgan would be held by the captain and first mate while their investigation was ongoing. Fire and gunshots would have to be explained. Morgan might even be detained until the boat reached Yuma, providing the *Gila* wasn't disabled or destroyed by the fire.

What about Hope—or Claudine—and her accomplice, Kirby Selinger? Would Morgan drag them into his own troubles? Or would they just play dumb and slip off the boat at Yuma and go their way. The image of Claudine, the actress, was burned into his mind's eye; he was certain he'd recognize her if they ever crossed paths again.

Charvein turned to look downstream, but saw no sign of the boat that had vanished in the distance behind some gentle rises of ground to the south. At least there was no red glare of fire or sparks rising into the night sky. Maybe quick work from the crew had doused the flames before they were able to spread.

Though he was stranded in an inhospitable desert, Charvein felt a great sense of relief. He'd kept his head and managed to escape. Taking inventory, he realized he had no food, water, knife or hat. But he did have several wax-coated matches that he habitually carried, and four twenty-dollar gold pieces—the remains of his pay from Pitney. He blew the excess water out of his Merwin Hulbert .32 and holstered it. The longer extra barrel was even in his pocket, with a handful of cartridges.

Except for a few bruises, he was in good shape. The skin of his wrists was chaffed raw and the rope had burned both sides of his neck. When he swallowed, it felt as if he had a lump in his throat, but he'd been able to grab the rope quickly enough to prevent any serious damage.

Flinging his wet shirt over one shoulder, he trudged away from the river in the bright moonlight, boots squishing. In a few hours, the sun would rise and he'd have other problems to deal with but, for now, life was a banquet. And there was nothing like a dash of danger to add zest to the feast.

CHAPTER 15

Lucinda Barkley was in the best physical and financial condition of her life—but she was miserable.

A cold sea wind gusted along San Francisco's Montgomery Street, billowing her cape and snatching off her hood. She turned her back to the blast, gripping the long cape, hair whipping around her face. Only another two blocks to the hotel. She was amazed it could be this cold in September, but at least she'd taken Sam Stonehouse's advice and bought some warm clothing. After her ordeal in the hot, dusty ghost town of Lodestar, she'd never anticipated being cold again.

The wind cleared her head and she began to regret leaving Stonehouse in that gambling den. He didn't drink when he worked at his profession, but she guessed a few winning hands of blackjack and Five Card Stud had made him reckless this night. He'd switched over to bucking the tiger where the odds of winning were much longer. He began to lose, but didn't seem to be practicing his usual caution. It was as if he were gambling with someone else's money—which he was. He was habitually careful and calculating, but, being flush with Ezra Pitney's gold was like playing with house money. She'd tried to stop him, or at least turn him back to poker, which required more of his skill and judgment.

She stood by his side, hissing a warning when he lost $500. Exasperated, he flung her away with a sweep of his arm, backhanding her across the nose. The stinging blow brought tears to her eyes. She staggered back, feeling blood begin to trickle from a nostril.

"No need for that, mister," a man next to Stonehouse had growled.

"Sorry. Didn't mean to . . ." he stammered. "Just wanted her away from me."

He actually did sound sorry, as if it'd been an accident, but Lucy was in no mood for his apologies. She'd had enough for tonight. She should have stayed by his side to puncture his inflated ego with sharp words of caution when he became reckless. But it was well past midnight, and she was beginning to sag. The swat in the face was the last straw. Besides, the smoky atmosphere was irritating her eyes, clogging her nose, and she needed to sleep.

Sam was a small-time gambler, she reflected as she hurried along the mostly deserted street. A week ago, when they'd stepped off the train in San Francisco, it hadn't taken long for the atmosphere of the golden city by the bay to go to his head like a snifter of brandy. After checking them into the Palace Hotel, one of the finest hostelries in the country, Sam fell to rubbing elbows with the truly rich. Lucy saw how it started to affect him, and it worried her.

By the time she turned into the lobby of the hotel, she was on the verge of turning around and going back. After all, she had her own interests to protect as well as his.

She hesitated in the lobby before starting toward the lift.

The clerk behind the long mahogany desk glanced at her curiously, so she picked up an abandoned newspaper from a leather chair and sat down, facing away from him, pretending to read.

Maybe it was time for a change. She'd hooked up with Sam to snatch the gold before Pitney could get to it. They'd barely succeeded. The thrill of a narrow escape, the flight in the wagon, the camping in the desert until they could reach a town with a railroad—had made them hard and lean as hunting wolves. But now the running and hiding and subsisting on short rations and few baths had given way to luxury—something she thought she wanted, but now found was beginning to pall. She stared unseeing at the ornate woodwork in the lobby, wondering what to do next.

If the pattern of the past week repeated itself, Sam would show up at dawn, half drunk, bragging of his small winnings, or sour about his losses. She'd help him out of his formal clothes and into bed, then adjourn to her own room next door to sleep until noon. At midday they'd rise and go downstairs to feast in the hotel dining room, where she consumed more than she ate during an entire day before they arrived here. It'd been only a week, but already the homemade breads, roast duck, oysters, fresh fish, vegetables and pastries were shrinking her clothes and making her short of breath when she climbed the city's steep hills.

If this lifestyle continued for a few more weeks, Sam, who was slowly losing the gold they'd managed to lug all this distance, would have them back on the street, broke, with no resources. Every day she tried to convince him to invest some of the gold or put it in the bank instead of the hotel safe. But he either ignored her or made vague promises of doing so later. His driving ambition in life was just what he was doing now— living like a king and gambling like a man obsessed. He never tried to approach her sexually. The girls in the saloons of Virginia City had this man pegged. His only passion in life was gambling—and now he had the means to indulge that passion.

When they'd escaped in the buckboard from Lodestar, they were carrying two gold bell clappers, three small ingots and a crude cross—just over a hundred pounds of gold, she estimated. Three nights later, miles away from Ezra Pitney and his two men who were stranded in the ghost town by the flooding playas, she and Stonehouse camped in the ruins of an adobe hut. Amidst the trash left by the previous occupant they discovered a rusty iron kettle half buried in the sand. Fallen roof timbers provided fuel enough for a hot fire and they began melting the two gold bell clappers and three ingots. The molten gold they poured into several narrow grooves fashioned in the smooth, wet sand. When the gold cooled, they chopped it into fragments of various sizes so it could be carried in their pockets, or several small leather drawstring bags they bought later. The cross they left intact, toting it in a cloth sack, planning to reduce it to small pieces with the axe when their other supply ran out. And that time was fast approaching if she was any judge.

Once they reached Carson City and felt reasonably safe from pursuit or detection, she'd suggested they split up the gold, and the money they'd obtained from the sale of the buckboard and mules, and go their separate ways. He'd demurred, offering some excuse. At the time, she was flattered he wanted to continue traveling with her. But she quickly realized it was her share of the loot he wanted. He never said so, but having access to her half of the gold would keep him going twice as long. Stonehouse was a reasonably nice-looking man, but she felt no attraction to him, and evidently the feeling was mutual. It was strictly a business partnership.

Now, she decided, it was time to sever that partnership

She got up and went to the desk. "Have the bellboy wake me at seven," she told the clerk, shielding her swollen nose with the newspaper. "Room 347."

"Yes, ma'am."

The lift carried her upstairs. She packed what clothes she wanted, then drew a hot bath. While the steaming water ran from the tap, she examined the puckered pink scar on her calf— the recently healed wound of a large-caliber bullet. Walking up the steep hills of this city she could still feel an ache in that leg, but considered herself fortunate to have escaped with no worse injuries from the gun battle at Lodestar.

But that was past history and she'd been generously compensated for her pain and trouble. In the foamy tub of water perfumed with fragrant oils, she soaked away the odor of cigar smoke from her hair and body. Every room in this expensive hotel had a private bath. It was a luxury she was going to miss.

"It's seven o'clock," came a male voice through the door.

From deep among the satin pillows, consciousness returned. "I'm awake. Thank you."

She got up and dressed in a divided riding skirt and cotton blouse, then pulled on soft, deerskin boots. Brushing out her dark hair, she secured it behind her head with a red ribbon.

For a good ten minutes she stood looking at the valises stuffed with new clothes she'd bought. It was more than she wanted to carry. A few minutes later, most of the clothes were back in the wardrobe. Some other woman in this chilly city could benefit from them. One small leather grip held a change of clothing, toiletries and a few essentials, but no identification of any kind. In case she got separated from her luggage, she kept a handful of small nuggets and small-denomination gold coins in the pocket of her skirt.

One last look around and she left the room, locking the door.

Stonehouse had to be in bed by now. She paused by his room and put an ear to the thin door panel. Muffled, regular snoring. So far, so good.

Tossing a tan duster over her arm, she took the carpeted stairs to the lobby. A new clerk was on duty—one she hadn't seen this week.

"I'm Laura Boniface," she let the assumed name roll off her tongue as if she'd been saying it all her life. "Checking out for a few days, and I'd like to take the valuables I've stored in your safe." She handed him the numbered receipt and her room key. "Yes, Miss Boniface," the tall, cadaverous man disappeared into a small room behind the counter.

She breathed slowly, trying to appear calm, hoping her demeanor excited no suspicions.

He returned in a minute, lugging the canvas sack with both hands. "Uh! Pretty heavy," he grunted, hefting it up onto the long counter.

"A valuable statue," she smiled. "Present for my aunt in Oregon."

She pulled the bag toward her and opened the brass latch with a key, rummaging around inside. "Here, you can put this back. I won't be needing it until I return." She handed him two of the small rawhide pokes containing approximately half the remaining gold she and Stonehouse had melted. No sense leaving him destitute. He would likely put himself in that position soon enough.

From her side pocket she drew several gold coins to pay for her room. She and Stonehouse had registered separately under different assumed names. *This place is really expensive,* she thought. Her parsimonious upbringing was hard to shake. The habits of a lifetime could not be thrown off in a few free-spending days. Although gold in all forms had flowed freely in this town for decades, they decided to avoid attracting any attention by stopping at a local bank to exchange the majority of their small, homemade nuggets for minted coins.

"Here's something for yourself for being so kind." She palmed an eagle and slid it into his hand.

The clerk broke into a toothy grin, totally incongruous with the rest of his face. "My pleasure, ma'am."

"Oh, and in case anyone comes asking for me, you haven't seen me. Understand?" She gave him her best smile.

"Exactly."

Ten dollars was a very generous tip, but worth it if it would also buy silence until she could get a long head start. Besides, there was plenty more, she thought, as she shrugged into the duster and swung the leather bag over her shoulder by the handle, trying to keep her balance. How much did this cross weigh, anyhow? Forty pounds? Probably a bit more with a couple of rawhide pokes of nuggets added in. She had to bow her back and lean forward to carry it.

Pausing by the front door, she dropped the grip and let the leather bag slide off her back. She was already panting and couldn't go too far with this load without help. But if she wanted to take the gold cross, it was the lightest she could travel. Maybe the doorman could hail one of the horse cabs along the street. But where to? A train would be the quickest and easiest way out of town. Stonehouse would also know that. Not bound for anywhere in particular, she sought to throw him off the track. What if she just rented a room in a cheaper hotel and hid out for a few days until he gave up looking?

But it would be foolhardy to carry this much gold into a cheap part of town where robbery and murder were daily occurrences—crimes that were committed for much less than was lying at her feet.

A clanging bell interrupted her thoughts as a cable car came along the cobblestone street. She didn't know where it was bound, but it would take her away from this hotel quickly. She hoisted her two bags and tottered out into the street where the car slowed and willing hands helped her up onto the step.

She smiled her thanks at the strangers as she took a seat, pulling her two bags under her feet. It would be best not to let too many people heft this particular bag to arouse curiosity about its weight.

The car rattled along for several blocks then started uphill at the same sedate pace of about seven miles per hour. She had to decide quickly where she was going. By noon Sam would awake and start looking for her.

When the cable car topped the hill and started down toward the bay, she suddenly had an idea. She could take a ship to the Sandwich Islands. It would be too easy for Sam to check the train depot and find out if she'd bought a ticket. He could continue to follow her. But a ship at sea was a safe haven from pursuit. Even if he somehow discovered where she'd gone, he couldn't catch up to her; it would be necessary to follow later on another vessel. She could always debark at some port other than the one she had a ticket for. That way, it would be much easier to lose him.

But potential problems cropped up in her mind. For one thing, she had no passport and carried no official identification. If she attempted to land in some foreign country, she'd have to declare her luggage, and the gold would be discovered. It would be confiscated and she'd be detained while inquiries were made to see if she was fleeing the law. If the vessel stopped at some remote Pacific island, she could jump ship. But the weight of the cumbersome gold cross would be a physical drag on her no matter where she went. And she certainly didn't want to be stranded on a primitive island where gold was used only for ornaments and didn't have the buying power it had in civilized areas.

If she somehow had the means to melt the cross or have it cut into small pieces, its total weight would be the same, and she'd have to manage it while traveling. And she would still have the problem of buying the silence of whomever she hired to cut it up for her. But if it *were* in smaller pieces, she could wrap them individually and mail them to General Delivery at some city post office and then travel in safety to claim them. Of course, that would mean letting it out of her hands, and there was always the danger of it being lost or stolen in the mail.

She'd acted in haste to be rid of Sam Stonehouse and taken the lion's share of the gold, but now the practicalities of escaping with the loot were beginning to overwhelm her. And it was too late to go back, even if she wanted to.

The cable car rounded a curve at the bottom of the hill and stopped to take on several passengers at the waterfront. She had to make up her mind quickly.

A nearby sign read:

Pacific Packet Line.
Fast, Reliable Steamship Service to Hawaii,
Australia & the Orient. Connecting Service to
Arizona Territory via the Sea of Cortez

The Sea of Cortez? That was the name of the gulf by Baja California. She quickly visualized a map of the area from her school days.

That was it! She wouldn't have to leave the country at all but could still get away by ship. Pulling her small grip and the heavy leather bag from under the seat, she stepped down from the cable car, dragging the one big bag behind her. She paused to breathe in the fresh morning air and feel the sunshine on her face for a minute until the carman rang his bell; the car gripped the cable and was off.

Then she muscled the burden up onto her back once more and walked heavily toward the steamship line office on the wharf. All the while she ignored the weight by trying to think up a good alias—one she could easily remember.

CHAPTER 16

Marc Charvein awoke to the irritating buzz of a fly around his right eye. He raised a hand to brush it away; his mind continued to drift upward from a deep canyon of sleep. Pushing up to a sitting position, he squinted at the daylight. His eyelids were gummy and he fumbled for his wet bandanna to wipe them.

The rising sun had topped a small hillock nearby; its rays beat down with a force he hardly thought possible this early in the day.

Crawling from beneath a large creosote bush where he'd slept the remainder of the night, he stood and brushed the sand from his damp jeans. The shirt he'd spread over the bush several hours earlier was nearly dry and he pulled it on.

Events of the night before slid back into focus. After climbing out of the water, he'd walked a mile or so eastward until the uneven terrain hid his moonlit view of the river. By that time the adrenalin had drained from him and he was drooping with fatigue. He'd sought out a large bush and soft sand, praying he wouldn't lie down on a scorpion or stinging red ants. He pulled off his boots, leaving his socks on, and lay down, fading into sleep almost immediately.

He was not about to cripple himself by walking in the desert with bare feet, so he sat down in the shade to wait while the sun and extremely dry air did their work of drying his damp boots. While killing time, he tried to form a plan of action.

Charvein calculated the *Gila* had traveled some sixty to

seventy miles before he decided the river was safer than the boat. It was likely too far to walk back to Ehrenberg. He was headed downriver anyway, so decided to continue south until he struck another human or a settlement. This was strange country to him, and he had no idea how far he'd have to walk to the next town, but he had to go on. There was no choice.

By mid-morning his clothes and boots were dry enough to be comfortable. And his body had dried out as well. He wished he had a hat, but realized he was lucky to still have his life.

Before starting on his trek back to the river, he removed the cartridges from his pistol and wiped off any remaining dampness. Then he tore off a small piece of his bandana and, using a twig, ran the patch of cloth through the barrel to be sure it was clear of sand.

His thick hair was fair protection from the sun, but he covered it with the large red bandanna tied under his chin like a woman's scarf.

He carefully stepped around the spiny prickly pear and cholla as he trudged west. The open terrain was scattered with creosote, ocotillo, Joshua tree and other desert plants. Layers of dun-colored rock protruded out of the sandy soil. Miles to the east low mountains humped up against the horizon.

Now and then he caught sight of a lizard darting into the shade. A lone hawk soared on the rising thermals far above him. Most of the night hunters had sought the shade of their burrows. The desert was silent. He guessed a light breeze might spring up as the ground warmed. He knew he was losing fluid, but his skin wasn't moist. His sweat dried as fast as it formed.

It wasn't long before the shining ribbon of water appeared ahead. When he reached the bank, he bent to scoop water into his mouth with cupped hands, opting for open water rather than the reedy marsh. It wasn't cool spring water, and left a good bit of grit between his teeth, but it was filling and provided life-giving moisture. He rinsed out the bandanna and tried straining the water through it. Better. And the cloth was cool when he put it back on his head.

He continued walking south along the riverbank, being careful where he stepped. Thank goodness there were no steep cliffs, bluffs or dropoffs to negotiate. Now and then he had to climb into and out of a dry arroyo that carried runoff from flash floods to the Colorado. But the terrain was mostly level and he fell into a stride that ate up the miles. By the time the sun was overhead he was ready for a rest. He hadn't eaten since his one and only meal on the boat, and his stomach was growling.

Pulling off his boots and socks, he slid on his bottom down the sloping bank and soaked his feet in the water as he rested.

Ten minutes later, he sensed a presence, although he'd heard nothing. He cautiously crept up the bank and looked around. A horse and rider were coming along the bank toward him from the north. He slid back out of sight and pulled on his socks and boots. Then he drew his pistol and climbed up far enough to see over a clump of cattails growing on the edge of the river. Charvein would make sure to surprise whoever it was. The horse came on at a slow, steady walk. Something seemed familiar about them. He squinted to see them more clearly.

Five minutes later, the horseman came close enough that Charvein suddenly had a jolt of recognition. It was his horse—the one he'd owned until yesterday when he sold it to the Indian boy in Ehrenberg—and the same boy was riding him.

With a great sense of relief, he holstered his gun and stepped out, waving his arms.

The boy reined up and stared, apparently wary. If he was armed, he made no move for a weapon.

The boy urged the horse onward at a slow walk. Finally, he said, "Señor Charvein? Is that you?"

"Yes. It's good to see you again. I had some trouble on the

boat and had to get off in a hurry," Charvein said in answer to the boy's unspoken question. "How far to the next town?"

The boy dismounted and for the first time Charvein noticed the young man had a short, stocky build. In middle age, if he lived that long, he'd probably have a tendency to put on weight. He thought the boy was a bit shy. Maybe he still felt the subservient attitude he'd acquired as a household domestic in the Army officer's family.

"About two hours from here. Not too far. But you are welcome to ride your horse, and I will walk."

"He's your horse now, Diego."

"But I will share him with you. You look tired."

"Gracias."

Diego looked at him, and Charvein knew the boy was probably speculating about what kind of trouble had forced him off the boat without even his hat. Diego's long, black hair was bound in place by a wide blue headband. The boy silently turned to his saddlebag, dug out a stick of jerky and offered it to Charvein.

"Thanks." Domestics and manservants were taught to anticipate the needs of their employers. But there was no servile attitude about this young man—no indication his action was anything more than kindness to a fellow traveler.

Charvein gnawed at the tough, salty jerky, trying not to show how hungry he was. "Where are you headed?" he asked around a mouthful of meat.

"The next village—Norton's Landing at the mouth of Red Cloud Wash," Diego said.

The two began walking side by side while the Indian led the horse. "I was told by a miner who came upriver to Ehrenberg that the Red Cloud mine is hiring. I must learn a trade and thought I would start there. I don't want to be a servant the rest of my life."

"I came from Nevada," Charvein said. "Heard there were mines in this district."

"Many types of ore," the boy said. "Mostly silver and copper. Even gold."

They walked in silence for several minutes. Charvein had assumed the young man didn't speak much English since he'd been rather quiet the first time they met. But he was mistaken. If Diego had been working as a domestic servant in the home of an Army officer and his wife, he'd either picked up good English there, or perhaps was a former student at some mission school. Charvein knew the Franciscans had been among the Yumas for nearly two hundred years.

The course of the Colorado began trending east, and Charvein noted a prominent peak thrusting alone above the skyline of low desert mountains about thirty miles ahead. "Does that peak have a name?"

"The white miners call it Castle Dome Peak," Diego said. "My people had a different name for it, but I forget what it is. Everyone calls it Castle Dome now. There are several mines over that way. The Yumas mined small amounts of gold many generations ago. But it was not used as money. Jewelry was made from it, and sometimes the jewelry was traded for other things."

For a few moments, Charvein stared at the distant, barren peak; it stood like a remote sentinel, its image wavering in the rising heat waves.

"Do you ever wish you'd lived before the whites came?"

"Never thought about that," the boy replied. "I was too busy trying to stay alive and earn enough to eat. My mother and father were very poor. I had four brothers and three sisters. Only three of us still live." He shook his head. "No. I don't wish for the old times. My people did not have the horse until the Spaniards came from Mexico. We are better off now." He grinned. "See what a beautiful animal I have?" He raised the reins in one hand. "He can carry me far and fast. Places I could never go afoot. I would never have such a gift in the old times."

"What did you name him?" Charvein asked.

"I call him Swift Hawk. He can fly over the ground with the speed of a hunting bird. And he has set me free of earth to fly with him."

"I see you treat him well and brought grain for this trip. He never had oats when I owned him." He smiled. For the first time since he'd sold this animal, he had no regrets.

The midday sun had heated up the desert, but it wasn't unbearable. Charvein estimated the days had rolled more than halfway through September by now, and that fierce orb was beginning to lose its intensity.

"Would you like to ride for a while?" Diego asked.

Tired as he was, Charvein shook his head. "I want to see you on his back. We can trade places later."

Diego mounted.

"You look like you belong there," Charvein said.

More than an hour later, Charvein squinted at two black spots in the distance by the river. "Are those the twin stacks of a riverboat?"

"Norton's Landing," Diego said, standing in the stirrups to get a better view. "Time for you to ride Swift Hawk." Diego dismounted.

Charvein swung into the saddle. The saddle felt strange and the stirrups were too short for him, but the horse's gait was familiar. It was nice to look between the ears of that bobbing head once more.

They entered the town and blended into a seething mass of people, horses and freight wagons. The place reminded Charvein of Virginia City during boom days but on a smaller scale. A steamer, *Mohave II*, was moored bow and stern to the sloping landing. Three sets of gangways led from ship to shore, the middle gangway about ten feet wide. A steady pounding underlay the general cacophony of noise. Charvein recognized it as the old familiar sound of a stamp mill working somewhere, crushing ore. It was a sound he was long familiar with. It made sense that a river port near many mines would have a reduction works.

The street along the river swarmed with pedestrians, men on horseback, but mostly wagons. A gang of laborers struggled to slide a huge piece of machinery down the middle gangway. A dozen ropes stretched taut to hold it from either side.

A steady line of men carried boxes, sacks and all kinds of smaller freight off both smaller gangways, loading them into waiting drays.

A man who appeared to be a foreman stood to one side, supervising. "Hey, boy!" he yelled when he spotted the short, muscular Diego. "You want a job?"

"Yes."

"Then jump in that line and give us a hand. I pay cash when the work's done."

"Watch my horse. I'll be back," Diego jogged away.

Charvein dismounted and stood looking on for several minutes. When it appeared the job of unloading the steamer would take a while, he led the horse to the hitching rail of a nearby saloon, secured him and went inside. It was about half full. Everyone from Norton's Landing and the surrounding mines must be in town today.

"I just hit town," Charvein said to the red-faced bartender. "Big crowd."

"Yeah. Unloading some hoisting machinery for one of the mines." He drew off a beer and slid the foamy mug toward Charvein. "Payday for some, too." The big man paused in his rush and mopped his face with a towel. "Smelter got flooded and part of it washed away last year," he said. "But they managed to rebuild most of it. A good bit of crushed ore going downriver to Yuma."

"Barkeep!" someone yelled, and the man moved away.

Charvein helped himself to what was left of the free lunch. Crumbled yellow cheese, a dill pickle and half-dried thick slices of bread. There was just enough food there to make him even hungrier.

A half-hour later he went outside and retrieved the horse just in time to see Diego take his pay from the foreman.

"Plenty of work here." Diego came up to Charvein, pocketing his small gold coin. "Foreman said I could probably find a job at the smelter. Might be better than trying to work as an underground miner."

"It would be for me," Charvein said. "Come on, I'm starved. I'll treat you to a steak dinner if we can find a decent place to eat. It took me a hunk of cheese and two beers to wash the taste of dirty river water out of my mouth."

Diego grinned.

The pair made their way along a line of parked wagons piled with sacked ore waiting to be loaded.

A shrill whinny like the scream of a cougar split the air a few yards away. Charvein jumped. Something had spooked one of the draft horses hitched to a wagonload of ore sacks. The big horse reared in harness and lurched sideways, pawing the air. A pedestrian dodged to avoid the flailing hooves. The driver was flung off the seat. The big horse came down on his forefeet, panicked and lunged forward, dumping off several sacks of ore.

Charvein flung Diego out of the way and faced the horse thundering toward him. Nostrils flaring, teeth bared, the animal loomed over him for an instant and he knew there was no escape.

CHAPTER 17

Charvein leapt for the bridle and caught it on one side, wrenching the horse's head sideways and down. But the animal jerked up, powerful neck muscles lifting Charvein and slamming him back against the horse's side, knocking the breath out of him. He clung desperately to the bridle with one hand and the reins below the bit with the other, feet bouncing along the ground as the snorting horse lunged ahead. He felt his ribs being pummeled, but dared not let go or he'd be crushed under the wheels of the heavy wagon.

His weight on the bridle began to slow the horse. Several seconds later, he heard shouts all around as men grabbed the runaway, bringing him to a stop. He let go and flopped to the ground, rolling away from the hooves, wondering how badly he was hurt.

"Charvein, you all right?" Diego's voice was near his head.

"I think so," he rolled over and pressed a hand to his side. He did a quick inventory. "Nothing broken." His pants were torn and his boots scuffed and he was sore, but apparently uninjured. Diego gave him a hand up.

Charvein took a deep breath. He was going to be sore tomorrow but, with any luck, he hadn't cracked a rib. One of the trace poles was split and Charvein wondered if he'd slammed into it. Four big men had the horse under control as the driver came running up.

"Thanks, mister."

Charvein nodded. "What spooked him?"

"Dunno."

"I saw the whole thing," another man said to the driver. "You were gabbin' with that teamster and the wagon just ahead of you rolled back into your horse."

"You saved my life," Diego said, his face solemn.

"Then we're even," Charvein said. "You snatched me out of the desert sun when I was lost."

Men slapped him on the back and pumped his hand. In the midst of all the noise, he caught the word "hero" several times.

"Thanks. Thanks. But I'm no hero. Just trying to keep myself from being run down." He slapped the dust from his clothes and edged away, taking Diego by the elbow. "As I remember, we were on our way to get a steak dinner."

"Why don't you let me buy you that steak?" another voice said behind him.

Charvein stopped. The burly foreman thrust out a hand.

"I didn't do anything," Charvein said. "Really."

"You'll find the best steak in town right over there," the foreman pointed a stubby finger at an adobe eating place with the name *MARTIN'S* crudely painted over the front door.

"Will you join us?" Charvein offered.

"I'm buying," the foreman said. "Name's Antone Belcher."

"Marc Charvein and Diego . . ."

The Indian smiled. "Just Diego will do."

"You're not afraid of hard work," Belcher said to Diego, falling in beside the pair as they worked their way through the crowded street toward *MARTIN'S*. "You two new in town?"

"He is," Charvein said. "I'm just passing through. How far is Yuma?"

"Fifty miles by river," Belcher said. "Don't want to poke my nose into your business, but if you're looking for work, I might have a proposal for you."

"Hope it ain't bustin' broncos." He pressed a hand to his sore ribs.

They reached the eating place and pushed through the door into a room that smelled of frying meat and chili peppers.

"Let's grab a table and I'll tell you." Belcher led them to a table near a window whose wooden shutters were open, admitting flies along with outside air.

They ordered steaks and potatoes. The tall waiter left and Belcher leaned forward on his elbows, glancing around to see if anyone was within earshot. "I like a man who's courageous and thinks quick," he began. "Can you tell me a little about yourself?"

Charvein felt his ears getting warm at this praise. "When I was younger I spent several years as a railroad detective," he said. "More recently, I had a few jobs freelancing, mostly as a lawman." He didn't go into any details about the Lodestar incident.

"Can you handle a gun? I notice you're packing a fancy pistol."

"Don't like to use it unless I have to, but I can hold my own."

"Mind if I take a look at it?"

Charvein hesitated for a split second, but decided to trust this man who'd been supervising the loading of the steamboat. He reached across to his left hip and drew the Merwin Hulbert, laying it on the table.

Belcher picked it up and carefully examined it. "Nickle-plated, ivory grip, rather small caliber. A woman's gun."

"It's a .32. I'd prefer a .38, but that's all the gunsmith had at the time."

"Looks new."

"Just bought it a few weeks ago before I left Virginia City. My old Colt .45 was about worn out."

"Ahh," Belcher said, as if that explained everything, and

Charvein wasn't some kind of dilettante.

"Gunsmith said these are the best-made guns he's ever seen."

"I'm not familiar with them."

"Let me show you how it works." He reached into his side pocket and produced the longer, 6-inch barrel. He proceeded to demonstrate how the barrels were interchangeable and how the mechanism slid apart to load and eject.

"Nice weapon," the bigger man said. "Good balance."

"I've only had to use it once in earnest," Charvein said, thinking of the wild encounter with Stripe Morgan where his only shot had missed.

"I won't ask the details of that." Belcher handed back the pistol and Charvein holstered it, wondering what all this questioning was leading up to.

The waiter arrived at their table carrying a tray with three plates of smoking steaks, mashed potatoes and beans. He left and returned two minutes later with three beers.

They settled in to eat.

"You married or have any close kin?" Belcher asked around a mouthful of food.

"No close kin. A few cousins back east."

"Ever handle a six-horse hitch?"

"Now and then. Usually no more than four."

Belcher drew a deep breath and leaned back in his chair.

"I hope you're not going to tell me you have some urgent business in Yuma or somewhere that can't wait."

"Actually, I was heading south for the winter to look for work someplace where blizzards aren't burying me up to my eyeballs."

Belcher grinned widely. "I think you're just the man I've been looking for."

"You've got my attention."

Belcher glanced at the Indian boy.

Charvein felt a flash of irritation. "You can tell him anything you can tell me."

Belcher nodded. "I'm in charge of the only two warehouses here. They're big. We handle nearly all the freight and supplies that pass through going to and from the mines in the Castle Dome Mining District east of here. A half-dozen freighters work for me, hauling food staples and small equipment to the mines. They're men I know and trust. Twice a month the Wells Fargo office here contracts with our company to send out the mine payrolls in the form of gold coin. I vary the schedule so there's no pattern, and the driver who gets the payroll doesn't even know until the day before."

Charvein figured there was some kind of danger involved or Belcher wouldn't have bothered to question him so closely. "Why doesn't Wells Fargo use their own employees for this?"

"Not enough full-time personnel. Cheaper for them to subcontract to me. The drivers are held to the same standard."

"The driver travels alone?"

"No. One helper assists with loading and unloading and functions as a shotgun guard."

"The driver brings stuff back from the mines?"

"Only small things. There's a bonus for the driver who happens to get the payroll. I usually do it by lottery."

"How much does it pay? And how long does the job last?" Charvein asked. His money was dwindling fast, and there was no point going on to Yuma where he might encounter Stripe Morgan again.

"Only two questions? I expected you to ask me why the last driver left the job."

"Don't care. The job's open. That's all that matters to me."

"It pays well, never fear. You've been a lawman, so you're used to dealing with risks. I'd never hire an inexperienced man to take this job."

"Inexperienced at what?"

"Trouble. The last man quit after a brush with the Indians."

"Indians?" Charvein arched his eyebrows.

"Bronco Apaches, I'm told. They still jump the San Carlos Reservation now and then while most of the cavalry is off chasing Geronimo and his band down in Mexico."

Something didn't quite ring true about this. "The San Carlos is a long way east of here. Apaches don't normally travel this far to raid, do they? And what would Apaches want with a payroll wagon?"

Belcher shrugged. "That's what was reported to me. I wasn't there and never saw them. Coulda been Pimas or Yumas, I guess. An Injun's an Injun, near as I can tell."

"The Yumas haven't robbed or killed since we fought the Spanish missionaries," Diego said.

"Oh, you a Yuma?" Belcher said. "Well, no offense. I wasn't accusing you. I try to judge each man by his own lights, and you weren't no slacker as a worker loading the boat out there." He turned back to Charvein. "Whether they were Apaches or not, I'm guessing they just wanted to take vengeance on any whites they could catch in some isolated place, steal whatever goods were in the wagon and cut the horses out of their traces to eat or sell. We use good horses, by the way." He sawed off a piece of steak and popped it into his mouth.

"Seems like mules would stand up better to this terrain and climate."

"Maybe. We use horses 'cause they generally have better dispositions. Not as balky. The mine owners hire their own teamsters to haul bulk ore down here to the stamp mills. They use huge wagons hauled by jerk-line teams of up to twenty mules."

"Why'd you ask if I could drive a six-horse hitch? The wagons that heavy?"

"Well, no. But I have a special project in mind." He pushed

back from the table and crossed his legs. "Two men who represent a group of New York investors arrived from Yuma on the *Mohave* today. They want to take a closer look at the mines near Castle Dome. I keep a coach for special runs. I want you to drive them."

"What kind of coach—a mud wagon?"

"Oh, no. It's a well-built Concord, modified to take the rough roads and washouts between here and there—swings on extra thicknesses of leather straps, has stronger axles. It's a light-bodied coach not quite as tall as the original Abbott Downing to keep it from being top-heavy."

Charvein began to wonder what he'd gotten himself into, but never let on. "I don't know the roads, so how can I be making a special run?"

"I'll send a shotgun guard with you who's very familiar with the area."

"Good."

"In addition to these investors, you'll be hauling this month's payroll for the six mines up there."

"Hmm . . . How heavy is the gold?"

"Not sure, but it won't amount to more than the weight of two more passengers. Those Concords look spindly compared to a wagon, but they can haul enormous loads."

Charvein nodded, recalling having ridden in stagecoaches when a dozen or more passengers managed to cram themselves inside and atop the coach, and even hung onto the boot. Fully loaded, Concords still bounced and swayed a lot, but could cling to muddy mountain roads or ride easily over narrow, gullied desert washouts, and rarely broke down. Concords were a marvel of design. And Belcher said this coach had been strengthened. Charvein lacked experience atop the box, but had taken the lines a few times to relieve the driver on long stage runs through the mountains west of Virginia City. He was confident he could do it. If something happened he couldn't handle, what was the worst that could happen? He'd be fired. He'd been fired before.

"I've always sent the payrolls with one of the freight wagons," Belcher went on, "so no one will suspect it's going by coach with distinguished visitors." He looked at Diego. "You didn't hear any of this conversation."

The Indian boy nodded, stone-faced.

"Might be a good idea if no one knows who these men are," Charvein said, thinking like a lawman.

"Too late for that. It's already been in the paper. That kind of news is big in a community that prides itself on development and growth. New investment, more wealth and so on."

"When do we start?"

"Tomorrow morning."

Charvein nodded. "I need to get a hotel and clean up. Buy some clothes."

"Make sure you get a good night's sleep. This run should take about a week, give or take." Belcher drained his beer and dropped a five-dollar gold piece on the table to include a generous tip. "I have to get back to work. The stage station is right on the main street out here. I'll see you there at sunup. We store our coach in their stable. Their hostlers will have it ready."

The three men rose to leave.

Things were beginning to fall into place, Charvein thought. After a long, lonely ride south through the California hills, only the near miss with Stripe Morgan had interrupted his plans for a winter in the warm desert. Now he'd fallen into a good-paying job in a remote part of the Territory where he wasn't likely to run into Morgan again.

Morgan and Pitney had tipped their hands, so Charvein would now be on guard. He was falsely accused of a theft, but couldn't prove his innocence.

And Pitney had a long reach.

CHAPTER 18

Carlos Sandoval pulled the canvas cover down over the packsaddle and tied it in place. His burro, Lupida, turned her head and regarded him with gentle, patient eyes as she flicked her long ears at flies in the still air. He chuckled and stroked her nose, then loosed her tether from the hitching rack in front of the Yuma Mercantile.

He'd bought enough staples to last a couple of weeks and paid for them with grains of gold the clerk weighed out on a delicate balance scale. He was slowly reducing three ingots of gold to usable crumbs. Those ingots he'd liberated from the stash in Lodestar would easily supply his meager needs for some time to come.

Although he'd recently become more comfortable shopping for supplies in populated settlements, he never lingered long in any town. Time and distance from western Nevada slowly eased his mind about being a wanted man. By now, the law had certainly given up looking for him. Many more serious crimes had long since claimed the attention of the law. Anyone who might be watching him now would likely take him for exactly what he'd become—a lone prospector scouring the desert hills for float overlooked or unclaimed by some mining company. He had two hours of daylight left and could be at least four miles out of town by dark, resting by a desert campfire.

Fastening the burro's long lead to the saddle of his riding mule, Jeremiah, Sandoval put a foot in the stirrup and was preparing to mount when his eyes fell on a tattered poster tacked to a board fence between the mercantile and a nearby saloon. Part of the heavy paper had been torn away and a corner was hanging down. But something about the block lettering looked familiar.

Stepping away from his mule, he pushed up the torn corner for a closer look. His stomach contracted:

> *CARLOS SANDOVAL*
> *WANTED FOR MURDER*
> Of a woman, Linda Sandoval
> And the Wounding of
> Deputy U.S. Marshal,
> Buck Rankin

This was followed by a crude ink drawing that bore only a vague resemblance to him. There was a printed description and then, in large lettering at the bottom:

> $5,000 REWARD—DEAD OR ALIVE

Sandoval looked around to see if anyone was watching, then tore the poster off the wall, quickly folded it and stuffed it inside his shirt. His heart was pounding, but he moved deliberately, casually.

He gathered the reins and mounted his mule. Leading the pack burro, he rode slowly north along the street. He glanced at the few buildings of old Fort Yuma on a hill across the river in California. He wondered if the army still occupied the place.

A stout trestle of timbers spanned the Colorado, supporting steel rails that glinted in the westerly sun. He rode downhill on the north side of the bridge, pondering how quickly the far reaches of this desert were being settled. Trains of the Southern Pacific could now travel from Los Angeles deep into Texas in only a matter of two or three days.

But none of this mattered to him. He'd become a solitary man. How different his course might be now if he and Linda had become the parents of a child or two. But, trying to protect her, he'd accidentally shot and killed his beloved wife, forever changing his life.

Sandoval was startled from his somber reflections when his mule suddenly stopped, blocked by a cluster of men spilling into the street from the riverboat landing.

Two crewmen of the steamer *Gila* were busy fore and aft, securing hawsers over iron cleats on the dock. A buzz of conversation rolled over three dozen curiosity seekers who crowded onto the wharf toward the damaged boat.

From his vantage point atop the mule on higher ground, Sandoval could see wisps of smoke curling from a gaping, blackened hole in the hurricane deck of the boat.

Several men and women on board crowded up to the edge of the deck, apparently anxious to debark with their luggage. The wide plank gangway was dropped into place and a crewman held back the passengers while a stout man with an official-looking badge glinting from his vest bustled aboard.

Sandoval watched the sheriff take custody of a prisoner in shackles and lead him off the boat. The man was disheveled and part of his shirtsleeve was torn away. What had he done? The lawman led his prisoner to the barred rear door of a horse-drawn van. On the side of the enclosed wagon box in sun-faded red lettering was painted *Yuma Territorial Prison*.

From only a few yards away, Sandoval viewed the hatless prisoner they shoved inside. A streak of white hair bisected the prisoner's head. Sandoval tensed with a sudden jolt of recognition. It was Polecat Morgan! There was no doubt about it. What was Ezra Pitney's bodyguard doing here? Sandoval vividly recalled eavesdropping on a conversation between these two in a Virginia City saloon only weeks ago.

The sheriff locked the barred door, rejoined his driver up front and the wagon pulled away.

Sandoval shifted in his saddle and started to urge Jeremiah forward when a slim young man pushed through the crowd and dashed up the gangway, bumping several shore-bound passengers. He braced the boat's captain by the rail and began talking, all the while scribbling in a notebook. After two minutes the animated conversation ended and the young man came ashore, shoving the notebook into his pocket.

"Hey, Josh, what happened?" someone shouted from the knot of men on the landing.

"Read about it in *The Sentinel*," the young man yelled back, not slowing down.

"Aw, c'mon!"

"A shooting. Man set fire to the boat. Damned near burned 'er up!"

"Was a woman involved?" another man cried.

"Anybody killed?" a man shouted.

The reporter just waved a hand and dashed away on foot, apparently rushing to make the next edition.

Sandoval sat still, his mind struggling to grasp the significance of this. He remembered Pitney's words. The mine owner was convinced Charvein had stolen his missing gold, and had ordered Polecat Morgan to give chase and bring it back. Had Morgan caught Charvein and killed him, somehow setting the boat afire in the process? And was Polecat Morgan now under arrest for murder?

He kneed Jeremiah away from the milling crowd and continued on his way. At first he considered camping at the edge of the mountains just east of town and riding back in next day to read the story in the *Yuma Sentinel*. He had to know if his old friend Marc Charvein was dead. But then the crinkle of his own wanted poster under his shirt decided him against it. He'd find out later. If Marc was dead there was nothing he could do for him now.

At the edge of town he gave wide berth to the squat stone buildings on a low mesa—the Yuma Territorial Prison. What a hellish place that must be! He cringed at the mental picture of being caught, convicted and locked up there to break rocks until he dropped dead of sunstroke or was knifed by some inmate. But there was no chance he'd wind up here, hard by the Colorado River. His crime had been committed in Nevada.

He carried the Colt Lightning pump rifle Charvein had given him, and his own Colt conversion, open top revolver, but kept both weapons concealed under his burro's pack. Few Mexican peasants would be carrying such weapons.

Once past the prison cemetery, he swung back to join the road that followed the riverbank north. Only his imagination was causing panic and the urge to hurry. No one had noticed him. He was wearing his straw hat and cotton canvas clothes and cord sandals of a Mexican peon, the outfit he donned when he came to civilization. With his dark skin, he blended in and no one in town had given him a second glance. It only seemed that way since he'd been startled by the wanted poster. He drew a deep breath to calm himself. There was nothing to be afraid of. The poster was torn and dirty and had obviously been there for many months. Deputy U.S. Marshal Buck Rankin was dead— shot in Lodestar by Lucinda Barkley to save Marc Charvein, after a wild shootout when half the town burned down. Was it possible that he, himself, could now be accused of murdering Rankin? No. Lucy and Marc were the only witnesses to that and neither of them would ever reveal what really happened.

Fleeing Lodestar had been his only option because Marc had gone home to report to Ezra Pitney, who would then come to claim his gold. Linda's grave was near that ghost town and he heaved a sigh, wishing he were still close enough to visit it. But life went on, and the dead were left behind.

How had this wanted poster wound up so far south? The killing of a woman in Nevada would surely not be important enough for such a widespread manhunt. It must have to do with the wounding of a Deputy U.S. Marshal. That was it. The Marshal's office in Virginia City had circulated the wanted fliers far and wide to every other Marshal's office in hopes of capturing a fugitive who'd shot one of their own.

He'd come south with the vague idea of connecting up with some of the cousins he hadn't seen in several years. Last he'd heard, one first cousin was in Tucson and one somewhere near Yuma. But the desire to look them up had faded when he arrived. Anyway, they probably thought he was dead by now. He'd see if he could prospect a little and then maybe try to find them later. But now, discovery of this wanted poster in Yuma made him want to stay out of town entirely, or be very circumspect when he did ride in for supplies. His earlier idea of trying to work for wages was not a good one either; he was apparently still wanted by the law.

Being a fugitive was not a comfortable existence. But, as long as he stayed away from people, he could relax. And the four years he'd spent hiding out alone in Lodestar had accustomed him to a solitary life. He'd be there yet if Marc Charvein and three convicts hadn't arrived to set off a fateful string of events.

He decided to ride northeast and angle inland in the general direction of Castle Dome. The Red Cloud mine was in that area, and it took out a lot of rich ore. There were some interesting geologic formations and outcroppings there, too. He might get lucky and discover a bit of color or pick up some rock float that looked promising.

CHAPTER 19

"I'm Marc Charvein." He thrust out a hand toward the bandy-legged shotgun guard striding toward him from the Wells Fargo office.

"Breem Canto," the man replied, eyeing Charvein with squinty green eyes. He passed Charvein, ignoring the proffered handshake. Like an agile monkey, he swung up onto the Concord's tall front wheel and settled himself on the left side of the box, tossing the short, double-barreled shotgun into the crook of his arm. "Let's get going," he said. "Sun'll be up in twenty minutes, and we need to make time while it's cool."

Friendly cuss, Charvein thought as he walked around the front of the team, checking the traces and making sure all lines were clear. He assumed the hostlers were experts at this, but deliberately took his time.

He glanced in the side window of the coach. "You gentlemen ready?"

"All set," nodded a tall, slim man in a gray suit.

Less than an hour before, the Wells Fargo clerk had introduced Charvein to his two passengers. Bud Archer, representing an upstate New York investment firm, seemed excited and nervous on his first trip west. He held a new-looking wide brim hat in his lap.

The passenger sitting opposite Archer answered to the name Keith Satterfield, a geologist from Phoenix, who'd been engaged to advise the investor. Satterfield, a chunky man with puffy red eyes, appeared to have spent more time over drinks than poring over ore samples. Comfortably dressed in tan canvas pants, vest and a loose white shirt, he wore a sweat-stained hat to protect a balding pate, but made up for lack of hair with bushy sideburns and a thick mustache.

Charvein had stowed their two valises in the boot, along with his own. The guard chose to drop his bedroll down under the front seat.

When Charvein had first arrived before dawn, the Wells Fargo clerk slipped him a large key and said, "Belcher and I stashed the box last night. It's in a special compartment beneath the floor. That's not locked, but the box is. You and the guard are the only ones who know it's aboard. You won't need to touch it until you get to the Red Cloud mine this evening."

Charvein took a pair of new leather gloves from under his belt and pulled them on. He climbed to his seat and, without looking at the guard next to him, unwrapped the lines from the brake handle and laced the leather reins between his fingers— three in each hand.

"Hyah!" He popped the lines over the team and the animals lunged ahead. The light coach leapt forward and they rolled out of town. Charvein let the rested, frisky animals trot for the first half-mile before settling into a walk. This coach had been cut down so it was about a foot shorter than the normal Concord. It had a more balanced feel without the leaning and swaying Charvein remembered.

He bent down the brim of his new hat against the rising sun. Amazing how a bath, shave and new clothes could make a man feel. Nine hours of sleep didn't hurt, either. The well-stocked dry goods store was able to supply even a suit of cotton long-johns, razor and toothbrush. New, short buckskin boots replaced the ones falling apart. He even bought a box of .32 cartridges gathering dust on a shelf.

"You say your first name's Breem?" Charvein said when Norton's Landing had been left behind and they were rolling along a long, flat stretch of road.

"You hard of hearing or somethin'?" the guard growled.

"Not a bit. But that's not your everyday name. How do you spell it?"

"B-r-e-e-m. Named after an uncle, Thomas Breem."

"Okay." He paused and glanced sideways at the profile of Breem. His nose had a hump that spoke more of violence than heredity. "Look, if we're gonna be on this coach for a few days, we might as well be pleasant and get along. No point in being grumpy. You go by Breem or Canto?"

"Breem'll do," he grunted.

Charvein made one more try at being social. "You been with Wells Fargo a long time?"

"I only do this when my other business gets slack."

"And what's that?"

"I bring in fugitives."

Charvein thought at first he was a marshal or a local lawman. "Oh?"

"Yeah. Some call me a bounty hunter."

Charvein's glance automatically went to the gleaming, blue-black Colt in the man's holster, then slid down to pick out the leather rifle case in the boot below.

"I see." Charvein kept his voice neutral. He had little use for bounty hunters, but it was a legitimate occupation—a dangerous, uncertain one, to be sure, but legitimate. Being a lawman had similarities, but bounty hunters worked for the reward, while lawmen kept the peace in other ways and worked for a salary. Too many bounty hunters he'd encountered were unscrupulous—hardly better than the men they tracked.

"I guess you don't approve," Breem challenged.

"What a man does for a living is his own business," Charvein said evenly, hands and forearms loose but sensing the horses. Almost automatically, his thumb and forefinger tightened slightly to guide the off-side leader into a long left-hand bend. The ease and pleasure of driving a seasoned team was coming back to him. He thought he could probably let them have their head and they would keep to the road with no trouble.

Charvein swept his gaze past the team to the winding road where it curved into a patch of hilly terrain a half-mile ahead. But his mind was on the small, bowlegged guard who sat swaying next to him, boot propped on the footrest. The feisty little man had a chip on his shoulder. Not very affable, but probably a necessary quality for a shotgun guard.

Hardly a word passed between the two men for the next two hours. The team slowed on an upgrade. When they reached the crest of the rise, Breem pointed. "Venter's Spring down in that bottom."

Charvein didn't see any sign of greenery, but took him at his word. When the team swung around the next bend at the bottom of the grade nestled between two hillocks, he saw a patch of green grass and willows growing in a swampy area about twenty yards square.

"Whoa!" The team halted at the edge of the pooled water and he set the foot brake, looping the lines around the handle.

Charvein climbed down stiffly and stretched. Breem was already taking out two of the canvas buckets to fill. "Ain't much of a spring," he said. "More like a seep this time o' year. But it's the only water between here and Red Cloud mine."

Charvein took the other four buckets and filled them, setting a full one by each horse.

Their two passengers got out to stretch their legs. Charvein noted that the geologist, Satterfield, was the only one of the pair wearing a gun. He guessed the investor, Archer, might have a pocket pistol tucked under his suit coat. Almost no one went unarmed in this country.

Breem immersed their blanket-sided canteens in the reedy water near the base of the spring. He brought the containers up by the straps, corked and hung two of them, dripping, on the box. The third he tilted up, drinking deeply, his Adam's apple working up and down.

Charvein took a long drink from one of the other canteens and handed the third to the passengers to share.

Twenty minutes later, after refilling three small water kegs, they were on their way.

After an hour, Charvein asked, "How far to the Red Cloud mine?"

"Only one road out here," Breem said. "You'll know it when you see it."

The sun was well down the western sky when Charvein swung the tired team in a wide circle and reined up at the Red Cloud mine. A cloud of fine dust caught up and settled over them. Each of the mine buildings scattered across the top of the hill near the hoisting works bore an identifying sign, so a stranger could easily find the office, the bunkhouse, the washhouse, the dining hall.

As he set the brake and swung down, Charvein was struck by the large area this place covered. He didn't know how much farther the underground tunnels might stretch. The place could hold its own in size with some of the smaller Washoe silver mines around Virginia City—except the Red Cloud mine was an isolated operation. As such, the company had to supply housing, food and a store for the three shifts of hardrock miners. Miners unhitched the team and led the animals away to be stabled and fed.

Archer and Satterfield shook hands with the mine superintendent who invited them for supper in the dining hall. Breem took his bedroll without a word and started toward the bunkhouse.

Charvein waited until the bowlegged man was out of sight before he pried up the panel in the floor under a coach seat and dragged out the heavy Wells Fargo box. His key opened the big brass padlock. The payroll for each of the six mines in the Castle Dome Mining District was in a separate canvas bag with the name of the mine stenciled in black on the side. He took the Red Cloud payroll and locked the rest back in the box and slid it back into its hiding place under the floor.

He delivered the bag to the office where the foreman was filling in for the superintendent. The foreman poured out the yellow boys on the desk, counted the gold coins, returned them to the sack and locked it in the office safe. Then he signed the receipt for Charvein. "I can't leave here just now, but you'll find the washhouse and the dining hall that way." He pointed over his shoulder. "And if you want, there are spare bunks."

"Thanks, but I'll sleep in the coach." It wasn't just to guard the money. He had no wish to share a bunkhouse with Breem or a group of strange miners. He'd been hired by Belcher to make sure this payroll money was delivered safely and that's what he intended to do. He took his responsibility seriously and decided not to let it out of his keeping, even to entrusting it to the mine office safe. He had no idea how many men had the combination to that.

He went to the washhouse and sluiced the dust off his hands and face at a hand pump. Then it was on to the dining hall for a filling supper of flapjacks, bacon and coffee. The grimy miners who came in eyed him curiously, but ate by themselves.

The superintendent was busy showing the investor and the geologist around and Breem hadn't reappeared, so Charvein went and stretched out atop the coach, watching the long, lingering September sunset and listening to the stillness. If this job always went this smoothly, he could relax and do it for several months or more. He knew that nothing was ever this easy for long.

Sunset faded to dusk and a few stars appeared. The moon illuminated the desert hilltop as darkness closed down. Even if these miners made good wages, this would be a lonely place to spend weeks on end, Charvein thought. But he assumed they probably devised their own amusements for the off-duty hours— cards, ball games, maybe something that didn't involve a lot of physical labor. He wondered if the mine tunnels had to be shored up like those in Virginia City. If so, the Arizona Territory mine operators also had to haul timber from mountains miles away.

Underground mining was an occupation that had never appealed to him in the slightest. Many experienced hard rock miners were recruited from Wales and Ireland and central Europe. Many were glad to escape poverty and oppression in their own countries and welcomed the good wages. Boredom and loneliness they could deal with compared to what they had left behind. The greatest dangers they faced here were endemic to deep mining—cave-ins, explosions, rock-dust pneumonia, being scalded with steam, broken bones from falls. And above ground, there were gunfights between drunken miners. Yet, this mine being isolated probably didn't allow liquor or women on the premises. When they got to town, they probably acted just like the miners in Virginia City who had all the pleasures and vices handy at the end of each shift. Many of those Nevada men went from week to month without saving a dollar of their $4 per shift pay.

Charvein sighed. Bad as being a lawman was sometimes, it certainly beat the life of a hard rock miner.

The desert air gradually cooled and a soft breeze caressed the top of the coach. It had been a long day. He put his head down on his crooked arm and dozed.

★ ★ ★ ★ ★

In his dream, Charvein slid from side to side on the box, the stagecoach bouncing and swaying beneath him. Where was the guard? Six horses were strung out in harness ahead of him and he held their reins. But the reins were loose. Too loose. He suddenly realized the lines were disconnected and the team was running wild. Tossing their heads, manes flying, snorting smoke and fire, the three pairs of devil horses thundered down the curving mountain grade, hauling him and the coach straight to hell.

The narrow ledge of road ran along a cliff on the left and a canyon on the right. Charvein slammed his boot against the tall brake handle and smelled the screeching brake pads burning against iron rims. The coach hardly slowed as it careened into a curve and tilted up on edge, inside wheels spinning free. Charvein lunged for the grab rail on the left. The Concord seemed to hang forever in its balance between time and eternity.

He heard himself scream as the coach was flung out into space and began to fall and fall . . . into the limitless gorge.

Charvein awoke, gasping, fingers scrabbling at the roof of the coach.

A nightmare. Had he screamed aloud? He actually felt the coach rocking beneath him. The lingering effects of the horrible vision? No. Something was inside the coach. He sat up. The coach tilted and he heard a grunt, then saw a man jump out and run toward the darkened mine buildings. As the figure passed through a shaft of light from the tin-sided hoist building, Charvein glimpsed a humped figure with a loping stride like some ape. Then it was gone.

Groggy from sleep, he scrambled down off the coach and gave chase. Sixty yards away he pulled up and listened for sounds of flight, but heard nothing over his own heavy breathing. He was in the deep shadows of buildings and saw nothing but blackness. He decided not to venture further. If there was no sound, the intruder had either made it to safety or had stopped and was poised for an ambush. Charvein didn't want a knife in his gut.

Charvein walked slowly back toward the coach. He didn't recall drawing his gun, but it was in his right hand. An instinct when danger threatened.

Someone after the treasure box? Word had probably spread among the miners that the payroll had arrived, and some brave or desperate soul decided there was more for the taking.

The Concord's right door stood open. Without striking a match, he leaned inside and felt for the cover of the compartment under the seat. It was loose, but the Wells Fargo box inside was intact, the brass padlock undisturbed. He put the lid over the compartment and shut the door. Somebody thought to catch him asleep, lift the heavy box and trundle it away to open at leisure. But who? Had this ever happened when they delivered the payroll by freight wagon? If so, Belcher hadn't mentioned it. The mine foreman who'd taken receipt of the bag knew it was here. And the shotgun guard, Breem, knew.

It could have been just about anyone. He leaned against the tall rear wheel, trying to recall his quick look at the fleeing figure. Short, bent over, with a strange gait like . . . like a bowlegged man might run. Very much like Breem. But there was no proof. Any number of miners he hadn't even seen could match that description. Should he ask the foreman in the morning which men were off duty and try to examine the miners to see if anyone fit his quick impression? A waste of time. Even if he found several of that general shape and size, there was no way he could establish the fact that one slipped out of the bunkhouse and tried to plunder the stage, apparently not knowing Charvein was asleep on the roof. *No, let it rest. Don't say anything to Breem in the morning.*

He climbed back to the roof of the coach and lay on his back, staring at the stars. There was no room to stretch out inside the coach. Thank God that nightmare had awakened him, or he might've slept right through the theft of about thirty thousand in payroll money.

He closed his eyes and tried to relax, but couldn't. He lay with his hand across his chest gripping his single-action Merwin Hulbert.

Chapter 20

Lucinda Barkley was sweltering in her cabin aboard the Pacific Packet, *Western Sunset*. She stepped out onto the deck for some air, automatically locking the door behind her. Going to the rail, she leaned on her elbows to stare idly down into the depths of the blue-green water. The ship swung at anchor off Port Isabel, Mexico, near the silted delta where the Colorado River debouched its reddish-brown water into the Sea of Cortez.

Two days before, the Pacific sea breeze had been blocked by the desert mountains when the ship rounded the foot of Baja California and steamed north into the gulf. The reflected sun off the calmer sea and off the zinc-covered decks heated the cabins like baking ovens. But the Baja peninsula also blocked the long Pacific swells that had roiled her stomach for the first several days out of San Francisco. She much preferred the heat. But the seasickness and the heat both robbed her of energy and appetite.

She spent as much time as possible on deck, but was always reluctant to wander out of sight of her cabin. The cross of gold that was hidden in its leather bag under her bunk was like a guilty secret. It was on her mind day and night. The cross had come to feel more like an anchor than a treasure—more like an instrument of crucifixion than a golden crown, the reward of all her efforts. She felt no guilt for possessing it; after all, she'd earned it. What she did feel was fear of its discovery. She was beginning to learn the constant pressure of being a fugitive.

Every passenger who looked at her more than casually—usually the younger men—seemed to penetrate her soul to discern the cache of wealth in her cabin. At least two shipboard flirtations were stopped short as a result of this fear. She'd read of an heiress who was being courted, but experienced an agony of doubt about her suitor, not knowing if his interest was in her or her inheritance.

And then there was Sam Stonehouse. She'd left him with the short half of the gold. But, if she'd stayed, they'd both be broke by now, considering how he was losing at the gaming tables. She constantly wondered if he was on her trail. It wouldn't take a great detective to find out she'd left by sea. Even though she'd bought her ticket under a false name, a description by Stonehouse would have identified her quick enough. *Never underestimate your opponent. I have to assume he's coming—soon.*

As a result of the weather, the worry over hiding the cross and the dread of Sam Stonehouse, her stomach was in constant turmoil. She was unable to eat more than a few bites at each meal, even though the ship's chef prepared some tasty fare. After two weeks, her unintentional diet caused her to grow thinner than she'd ever been in her adult life. The weight she'd begun to pick up in San Francisco melted away, and she found herself pinning the skirt waists to take up lost inches. The few new clothes she'd managed to bring stayed in her valise.

She stared moodily into the water, accommodating herself to the slow heave and roll of the anchored vessel.

Lucy was glad this wasn't a large, luxurious ocean liner with maids. Any cleaning lady probing under the blanket that hung down over the edge of her bunk would immediately discover the heavy bag with its gold cross. But denying access to her cabin might have aroused suspicion. Thank goodness, all the passengers aboard the *Western Sunset* were left alone to keep their own quarters in order.

Supper was being served and the delicious aroma of fried onions wafted from the galley.

She tore herself away from the rail and, with one last glance at her locked cabin door, went into the saloon. She hadn't had a proper meal for several days and really needed to eat while she was hungry.

Ten minutes later she was digging into hot mashed potatoes, fried corn and tender, fresh sea bass. About forty passengers crowded the dining area and the hum of conversation filled the room.

"Ladies and gentlemen!" a voice cried at the far end of the room. "Please, may I have your attention for a moment."

Heads turned toward the forward end of the dining hall.

"I have an announcement."

The conversation slowly died. A bearded man was standing on a chair holding up his hands for quiet. It was Captain Adolphus Green.

"Word has just reached me through the Mexican harbor master that the *Gila* has been damaged in a fire. All of you were scheduled to transfer to that river steamer here at Port Isabel to carry you up the Colorado. But the *Gila* is laid up at Yuma for extensive repairs."

The crowd groaned as one.

"Don't worry. The company is sending down another boat to pick you up, but it might be at least three days before it arrives. The crew and I will do all we can to make you comfortable until it arrives. If any of you would care to go ashore in the meantime, you are welcome to do so. The authorities here don't require passports."

A general hubbub of complaining broke out among the passengers.

"I know, I know." Captain Green raised his voice over the tumult. "I'm as frustrated as you are. After more than two weeks, I'm sure you're anxious to get off this ship and continue your journey. And I'll be thrown off my schedule returning to San Francisco because the *Western Sunset* was due to take on passengers and freight from upriver." He shook his head. "But things like this—and the weather, of course—are unpredictable and beyond our control." He stepped down off the chair. "I'll keep you informed as I get word." He left by the forward door.

The delay meant little to Lucy. She had no plans. In fact, she still hadn't decided what to do when she reached Yuma. To get completely clear of Sam Stonehouse, she'd nearly made up her mind to take a Southern Pacific train east as far as the railroad went into Texas. She had to take every precaution to throw Sam off her trail. And she had no doubt he would come after her. When she'd partnered up with that compulsive gambler to take the gold, she'd grabbed a badger by the tail, and now found she couldn't safely let go. Even if they'd signed a written agreement, instead of a verbal agreement, to divide the gold evenly, she doubted he'd have stuck to the contract once his gambling/gold fever got the best of him. They should've split the take and gone their separate ways immediately after escaping from Lodestar.

She quickly finished eating before the heat-induced feeling of nausea returned.

Going on deck, she paused in the shade, relishing the slight land breeze. The captain had said anyone could go ashore to kill time. Could she chance it? Then a sudden thought occurred to her.

The captain came along the walkway and started up the outside ladder to the next deck.

"Oh, Captain Green!"

The mustachioed officer paused and leaned over the banister. His white shirt was damp with sweat. "Yes, miss?"

"Will another ship be arriving here soon from San Francisco?"

"As a matter of fact, the *Delta Fisher* is due four days from now. We might pass each other as we start south. Why do you ask? Expecting someone?"

"Actually, a friend and I were going to meet in Yuma. I thought perhaps he would arrive here on the next ship, and we could travel upriver together."

"Knowing how some of these delays last longer than predicted, it's very possible you'll meet here."

She forced a smile, hoping it appeared genuine. "Thank you, sir."

He nodded and continued up the steps.

Lucy's stomach contracted and she had to take a deep breath to keep from throwing up over the railing. The fates were conspiring against her. In spite of all her plans, it was highly likely that Sam Stonehouse would catch up with her before she could escape. He would have had plenty of time to figure out where she'd gone and book passage on the next ship.

She walked slowly down the deck to the fantail of the small vessel and scanned the sun-drenched port. What to do? If he caught up with her, she could claim she'd only taken her share of coins. But he knew she'd taken the cross and would demand she give it up. She was just stubborn enough that she wouldn't do that. It was her idea to go after the gold in Lodestar. *She* had recruited *him*. She was still the boss. If she saw him coming and dumped the cross overboard, he'd never believe she'd thrown something that valuable away. In spite of the bribe she'd given the hotel clerk to keep quiet, Stonehouse would have raised enough hell with management to force out the truth. He'd discover she checked out with most of the sacks the pair had left for safekeeping. No, there was no way she could lie her way out of this. She had to avoid Sam Stonehouse at all costs. But how? She was trapped aboard this ship. He'd beat her or apply some kind of torture until she revealed the whereabouts of the cross. If she dumped it into the sea, he'd likely be so furious he'd make sure she disappeared overboard as well.

Troubled, she stood staring at the fishermen's boats that were coming in from early-morning trips and beaching on the white sand to unload their catch. To take her mind off her own dilemma, she wondered what kind of life those fishermen had. How far out did they have to sail to make a good catch? Did each man have a favorite spot? With the competition, did each boat earn enough to support one or more families? It was likely the fresh sea bass she'd had for lunch had been caught by one of these men. Surely, they also sold to passing ships and riverboats, besides just the locals.

Thin, high clouds passed over the sun briefly. Then the sun burst out again, reflecting off the white sails of the small boats. Like the brilliant light reappearing, an idea flashed into her mind. Her heart beat faster. Did she dare try it? A desperate plan, to be sure, but it just might work. She turned and went quickly to her cabin.

Changing into her riding skirt, she donned a white cotton blouse, vest and broad-brimmed hat. Soft, short doeskin boots completed her outfit. Should she wear the dark green glasses she'd bought to protect her eyes from the tropical sun? No. The Mexicans might think she was putting on airs.

She went on deck and joined eight men and women who'd gathered near the port bow, preparing to go ashore for the afternoon.

The crew had arranged for a launch to come alongside and take the passengers ashore for a few hours of sightseeing and shopping for local crafts. The others consisted of four couples, all of whom appeared to be older than she.

With the assistance of a deckhand, she stepped through the opening in the rail and down into the twenty-foot boat that a Mexican held against the bow of the ship.

During the row ashore, she savored the smell of the fresh salt air, the breeze and the sunshine. Maybe she should spend the winter here. But Mexico was as lawless as Virginia City, and she didn't speak Spanish. A white woman alone would be an easy victim.

The passengers dispersed up along the beach, strolling into open-front stores to gaze at fresh fish, vegetables, baskets, straw hats, seashell jewelry and hundreds of other items she had no interest in.

Pretending to shop, she fingered a pearl necklace.

A young Mexican woman came to wait on her.

"Do you know those fishermen?" Lucy asked, nodding at the boats pulled up on the beach a hundred yards away.

"*Si*, I know them. One ees *mi hermano*."

"Your brother?"

"*Si*. He is one of the best fishermen. He has his own boat, which he built with his own hands."

"This is a most beautiful necklace."

"It would look very nice on you, *señorita*."

Lucy unhooked the clasp and turned around so the lady could fasten it behind her neck. "Are these local pearls?"

"*Si*. Oysters come from our sea just out there." She pointed with her chin.

"How much?"

The lady quoted a price that was probably more than the string of pearls was worth, but Lucy paid it in tiny one-dollar gold coins without comment.

"Does your brother ever take travelers for rides in his boat?"

"I'm not sure," the lady said. "Do you wish to wear the necklace?"

"Yes. It's beautiful."

The Mexican woman glanced toward the beach. "I could ask him."

"You would be very kind to do that. Our ship has been delayed here a few days," Lucy explained.

"Where do you wish to go?"

"Oh, out into the gulf a few miles to enjoy the sailing. Maybe he'd teach me to fish."

"Are you here alone?" The Mexican woman seemed a bit suspicious.

"Yes. I'm traveling for my health, but plan to meet my fiancè in Arizona." Lucy looked toward the beach where the gray/white gulls were circling raucously overhead, looking for a meal. "Which one is your brother?"

"The one on the left there—seated on the bow working with the lines."

"I see. Does he fish alone?"

"Sometimes he takes another boy with him to help."

"I think it would be fun to take a ride up the river."

"That would be difficult against the current."

"Has he ever done it?"

"I do not think so. There is nothing that way but the red water and fifty miles of desert to the border."

"I would like to see it up close. If the river is wide enough in places to tack against the current, or if he could row, or tow the boat by walking along the bank . . . I would love to see some of your beautiful Mexican desert. I live in San Francisco where the weather is always cold and foggy."

The Mexican woman seemed dubious.

"I will pay him well for his trouble, if he could give up a day of fishing."

The lady smiled. "My name is Juanita, and my brother is Victorio. May I tell him your name?"

Lucy had to react quickly with the pseudonym she'd been using aboard ship. "I'm Carmen Lucas," she held out her hand with a smile.

"I will go call him." Juanita instructed her small daughter to watch their stand and went off to summon Victorio.

Thirty minutes later, Lucy had made arrangements with Victorio to transport her upriver on a sightseeing jaunt.

"The current won't be too strong for you to pole or row?" she asked when they'd settled on a price.

"No *señorita,* not at all. I can do eet." He thrust out his bare chest as if to impress this pretty and wealthy woman.

"Row to the steamer before dawn so we can get an early start," she said. "I want to take two bags with me. I'm afraid to leave them aboard the ship while I'm gone."

"*Si.* I will be there."

"Good. I'll be waiting near the port side just before it's light enough to see. Here is something for your trouble. I'll pay you the rest later when we return." She put a five-dollar gold piece in his hand.

CHAPTER 21

Marc Charvein sat on the driver's box at sun-up next morning, reins in hand, waiting for the signal to get underway.

"Red Cloud is a very stable mine," the superintendent said to Bud Archer. "As your geologist, Mr. Satterfield, has seen, the strata here shows our deposits of silver and veins of gold ore are likely to last for years to come. Not one of your average boom-and-bust operations."

The tall, lean tenderfoot climbed into the stage and the superintendent slammed the door. "A good mine for your investors," he stated as a parting shot of salesmanship. "There's virtually no risk in buying stock in our mine."

Archer tapped the breast pocket of his suit coat. "I have all the figures written down and will certainly present them to the board."

The mine superintendent stepped back and waved to Charvein who popped the long whip over the backs of the horses. The team lunged ahead, jerking the stage into motion. They rolled down the slope onto the road and headed north toward the next mine. They were away and Charvein settled himself for another long day.

Breem, the bandy-legged shotgun guard, slouched on the seat beside him, surly as ever. They'd only nodded to each other this morning in the dining hall, then went to sit apart among the off-duty miners.

Charvein's eyes were gritty from lack of sleep and he wasn't looking forward to another day of dust and sun to further irritate them.

He'd gone over the incident of the night before until his brain wearied of it. But he came up with no explanation of who or why someone had climbed into the coach in the dark, then run off when he realized Charvein was sleeping on the roof. There was nothing of value inside except the padlocked Wells Fargo box containing the payrolls for five more mines. Reason enough for a midnight foray, he guessed. Charvein almost regretted not chasing the intruder into the black shadows of the mine buildings. But blind pursuit could have proven deadly, if the man was more than just a casual thief.

He held the lines loosely and gave the horses their head as they trotted down a long gradual slope out into the early morning. The sun was just up and beginning to warm him, after a rather chilly night spent under the stars. The desert smelled fresh and he inhaled deeply. Sure beats working in an office or some store.

The guard sitting next to him was certainly not an affable man, Charvein thought. Breem chose to keep to himself. Probably a good thing. Chatty traveling companions could wear on the nerves after a few hours. It was better the guard tend to business and stay alert, although the peace of the desert landscape belied any danger.

The Carbuncle was the next mine, twenty-five miles to the north. Then, tomorrow and the days to follow, he'd swing the stage to the west and south to deliver payrolls to the last four smaller mines in the string of six.

Since there was no hurry, he took it easy on the horses. Best to make sure they had no accidents, since there were no stage stations out here to provide replacements should a horse throw a shoe or step into the burrow of a kangaroo rat.

Breem broke his silence to tell him there was exactly one

small stream five hours ahead.

"All the cricks hereabouts dry up this time o' year," he volunteered, although Charvein was aware of that. "This one don't, but it does flow underground for a couple miles."

The day before at the spring, they'd filled not only their canteens but topped off two water kegs they carried in the boot, just in case the next waterhole was dry. Belcher, the foreman at Norton's Landing, had mentioned these six mines drilled deep enough to strike water, supplying enough for their needs. It was the scarcity of water in the surrounding desert that made travel difficult.

Charvein kept the horses to a walk and stopped every hour or so to let them have a breather. There was nothing to graze on during the fifteen-minute stops, and he didn't want to water them yet.

At half past one that afternoon, they topped a slight rise of ground and Charvein spotted a streak of green in the distance, winding through a groove in the desert. But it was another hour before they came within a hundred yards. A bosque of trees marked the unseen watercourse.

The horses could smell the water and picked up the pace to a trot. Charvein let them go. "I don't reckon the water has gone underground," he said aloud, "or they wouldn't be so eager."

Charvein braced his boots on the footboard as the Concord rocked fore and aft, listening to the steady rumble of hooves, wheel rims grinding and trace chains rattling.

When they approached the trees near the ford, he reined in slightly and swung the team off the road, guiding them into the shade of the big cottonwoods.

A volley of rifle fire ripped the stillness, bullets splintering the footboard.

"*Hyah! Hyah! Git!*" Charvein grabbed his whip from its socket and snapped it over the team. Its popping noise was lost in the cracking gunfire. Charvein saw muzzle flashes in the shadows. The tired team lunged ahead in full panic, bursting into a dead run. The stage reeled after them as they burst from the shade into blinding sunlight on the other side of the grove.

Two Indians afoot on each side of the coach were firing as fast as they could lever their repeaters. The coach left them behind.

Charvein tried to swing the leaders sharply right. Iron horseshoes rang on stone. The coach hit the level ford, wheels spraying sheets of water to both sides. But they were turning too fast and the off wheel of the coach slid on mossy rock and chunked down into wet gravel. The horses were yanked to a stop. Charvein was nearly thrown off the box.

BOOM! BOOM! Breem flung himself back across the roof and let go with both barrels of his shotgun.

Charvein dropped the reins into the foot well and slid down himself, yanking his pistol. He was suddenly conscious of gunfire coming from the coach windows below. Charvein spotted only four Indians. Four against four. Two of the attackers were now back on their horses. The other two were splashing across the stream, firing as they went.

Breem dropped the shotgun and reached for his rifle sheath in the front boot.

Bullets thudded into the wood near Charvein's head. He thumbed back the hammer and snapped off a shot at the nearest Indian twenty yards away. His second shot clipped a brown leg, staggering the figure in the breech cloth. But the attacker sprang to the bank and dove behind the bole of a thick cottonwood. Had the Indian just lost his balance in the knee-deep water, or was he actually wounded? Charvein swore. Maybe this .32 was too small a caliber.

Charvein crouched in the front boot. Breem lay prone on the roof, firing his Winchester, but then spun around to get off three shots at the two mounted Indians who'd ridden uphill past the coach, shooting wildly over their shoulders as they went.

Four Indians in all, Charvein thought, two of them circling on horseback, the other two crouching behind trees along the stream. He fired at the nearest behind a tree, his bullet knocking chips of rough bark from the trunk.

Something struck the thin wood of the boot in front of him. He gasped as the bullet came through and burned across the top of his shoulder. It barely cut the skin, but he glanced down and saw his cotton shirt reddening with blood.

Charvein thumbed back the hammer and balanced the barrel of his Merwin Hulbert on the lip of the boot. Holding his breath, he focused on the spot where the rifleman was crouched. The Indian thrust the barrel and part of his head around the edge to fire. Charvein squeezed the trigger. The rifle flew up in the air and the Indian fell back with a yell.

"Hit sumpin'," Charvein muttered.

Shouts and gunfire continued. Whirling chaos around him as the mounted Indians thundered past the coach firing their carbines one-handed while they leaned low over their horses' necks.

The panicked team, trapped in harness, were squealing, whinnying and walling their eyes. The coach was stuck, and one of the wheelers had been hit and was down.

Breem was still firing at the two on horseback, but the targets were too fast and elusive.

The boom of a big-caliber rifle gradually began to penetrate Charvein's consciousness. Another attacker, shooting from a distance?

He glanced quickly around, but saw nothing. Then he heard the distinctive boom again and saw a puff of smoke from an outcropping of rock a hundred yards away. Then another, and another.

One of the mounted Indians went down, his horse cartwheeling, pitching the rider over its head into the creek.

Someone else on the hill had joined the fight and began tilting the odds in favor of the men in the coach. The downed rider sprang to his feet, unhurt, and clambered up behind the other mounted Indian who splashed into the water and reached down for him.

The third Indian, afoot, grabbed for his tethered horse in the thicket. The attacker Charvein had fired at limped away with desperate speed. He yanked the reins loose and vaulted onto the bare back, kicking his mount into motion. The three horses and four riders thundered away through the thick growth.

Charvein's pistol clicked on an empty chamber. Breem sat up.

Two parting shots came from the unseen rifleman on the hill, then silence settled over the scene.

Charvein swallowed and found his mouth and throat dry. He struggled up out of the front boot. "Anybody hit?" he yelled down to the men inside the coach.

The door opened and the two passengers came out, the easterner holding his arm, looking pale and disheveled. Satterfield thrust his revolver back into its holster. "Archer took one in the arm."

Charvein looked toward the hill again but saw nothing. He climbed down from the box, knees so weak he had to hold onto the rim of the front wheel to steady himself.

Breem, red in the face, knelt on the roof, slipping cartridges one at a time from his vest pocket and thumbing them into the loading gate of the Winchester. "Damned 'paches!" he gritted between clenched teeth. "Skedaddled."

"How bad is it?" Charvein guided Archer to the step of the

coach so he could sit down. Charvein helped him out of his suit coat. The sleeve of his white shirt was soaked with blood. To his inexpert eyes, it appeared the bullet had broken one of the bones of the forearm, but apparently missed any arteries. "Here," he said to Satterfield, "tear off a piece of that clean shirt and bind up his arm. Looks like the bullet came out the back. Oh, you got any whiskey on you?" he added.

Satterfield reached into a deep inside pocket of his vest and produced a silver flask.

"Pour a little on the wound and then give him a shot. Have him lie down inside before he passes out."

"Who the hell was shooting from the hill?" Satterfield used his sheath knife to cut off the other sleeve of Archer's shirt for a bandage.

"I don't know. But he sure saved our bacon." Charvein took a deep breath, beginning to feel the blood come back into his face. He glanced at the body of the Indian's horse that lay in the water. Then he went to the front of the stage where the wheeler lay dead with a bullet hole in the head. He walked around the rest of the team, talking calmly to them, running his hands over their quivering necks and flanks.

"One of the wheelers is dead," he said to Breem as the guard stepped down, still holding his rifle. "You hit?"

"No, but you are," he pointed at the bloody shirt. Charvein was suddenly conscious of the sting on top of his right shoulder. "It's nothing. I'll tend to it later." He turned to take a good look at the bosque of trees, the creek, scanning the open land to be sure the attackers were gone. "Look," he turned back to Breem and Satterfield, "the three of us will have to unhitch and get the dead horse out of harness. We'll go with a team of four, and trail the other wheeler behind the coach for now." He wondered what awaited them down the road. Would they make the Carbuncle mine without further trouble? Were other Indians waiting to ambush the weakened party?

"Hello, the coach!" a voice cried.

Charvein and Breem swung around toward the sound, the guard bringing up his rifle.

"Hold it! Hold it! I'm a friend."

A man stood at the crests of the rise above the creek, holding both arms in the air, a rifle in one hand. His face was shadowed by a straw hat.

Breem lowered his rifle, but Charvein kept a hand on his holstered revolver. "Put your rifle down and walk down here," Charvein ordered. The voice sounded vaguely familiar, but Charvein wasn't trusting his memory at the moment.

The man placed his rifle on the ground. Keeping his hands in plain sight, he walked slowly down the incline toward them. "That was me shooting from the rock up there," he said as he approached. "Heard the gunfire from over the hill. Thought you could use a little help when I saw the situation."

Charvein knew that voice. "Carlos Sandoval?"

"Marc? Marc? By God!"

Both men removed their hats so the sun shone fully on their faces.

They locked briefly in a bear hug.

"Never thought I'd see you again!" Charvein held the smaller man at arm's length. "A little leaner, a little darker, but still the same. How's the arm?"

"Healed up. The more I use it, the stronger it gets."

"We gotta have a long talk when we get time. Right now, we have work to do. Can you help us?"

CHAPTER 22

Bud Archer lay on the floor of the coach, his arm bandaged and a wet bandanna on his forehead while the other four unhitched the team and struggled to remove the harness from the dead horse. That done, Charvein and Breem led the five remaining horses upstream a few yards to drink. Then they tethered the team to two small trees with the long reins, giving them freedom to browse on scant grass and leaves of nearby bushes.

Charvein leaned on a tree in the shade and wiped his face with his sleeve. "Could've been a lot worse,' he said to Sandoval. "Two horses dead, one man wounded—or two if you want to count this flea bite on my shoulder. Except for a lot of bullet holes, the coach seems all right. We'll know for sure when we pull that left front wheel out of the gravel."

"Any of those Indians hit?"

"Possibly one with a leg wound." He paused and brought up an image of the wild scene. "It does seem a little strange there weren't more wounded or killed. A lot of lead flying."

"Everybody excited—and they were moving," Sandoval said. "Speaking of shooting, let me get your rifle I laid down up there." He jogged back up the slope and retrieved it.

"My rifle?" Charvein said.

"Yeah. See?" He held up the Colt Lightning pump. "The one you gave me."

"It couldn't have gone to a better man," Charvein took the Colt Lightning pump and looked it over.

"More modern than my Henry," Sandoval said. "But that was still a good rifle, too. I gave it to *mi amigo* in Virginia City for hiding me."

"Yessir, like meeting an old friend," Charvein noted the well-oiled weapon and polished wood. He handed it back. "And, speaking of old friends, it's like a miracle seeing you here."

"Providence, maybe, if not a real miracle."

"Providence or fate or something besides plain luck. There's a reason you showed up when you did."

"I was prospecting the other side of that hill and heard the shots," Sandoval said. "In this country, I can't range too far from water with my animals."

"You still have Jeremiah and Lupida?"

"Yes. Don't know what I'd do without them."

"So, you saved my life again."

"You probably could've held 'em off," Sandoval demurred. "But I helped tip the balance a little."

"Mind giving me a hand untangling this harness?"

As the two men worked, Breem walked up out of the wash to scan the surrounding country for any further sign of trouble.

Satterfield examined the coach. "We're in luck," he called to Charvein. "No broken spokes, and the axle isn't cracked. Should be okay once the team's hooked up again. They can pull us out of this hole."

"Any idea what those savages were after?" Sandoval asked Charvein.

"That's what I'd like to know. The man who hired me at Norton's Landing said one of his freight drivers quit after a brush with Indians. He thought they were Apaches."

"I had a good look through my field glasses," Sandoval said. "Strangely, they *did* look like Apaches—small, wiry, wearing the breech clout and those high desert moccasins, long hair with headbands. But when I lived in this Territory eight years ago, the Chiricahua, the Mimbres and other bands operated farther east of here."

"The cavalry out of Fort Huachuca is chasing Geronimo and his bunch down south in the Sierra Madre right now," Charvein said. "Could be a few more renegades got tanked up on *tiswin*, jumped the reservation and went looking for any whites to take it out on. Maybe steal a few horses along the way."

Sandoval nodded. "By raiding out here, they're farther from the nearest Army post. And they could be over the border into Mexico before anyone got word to come after them."

Charvein looked around to locate Breem, then said softly, "I reckon they have no use for the payroll we're carrying."

Sandoval shook his head. "You're wrong. More than twenty years ago, Apaches learned the value of the yellow metal. They trade it for anything they want, but can't steal."

"Could be, some white man put them up to it." Charvein spoke so quietly only Sandoval could hear.

"You think so?"

"Just a thought," he muttered, nodding his head slightly toward Breem.

Charvein was burning to ask his friend one big question, but dared not bring up the subject of the missing Lodestar gold just now.

Breem came back from the top of the wash.

Charvein noted the Marlin carbine he carried. The guard obviously took good care of it and brought it along to supplement the double-barreled shotgun that was standard issue for Wells Fargo guards. Breem was either a notoriously bad shot or maybe his weapon had a bent sight. But, for some reason, during the two minutes of the attack, Breem, lying prone atop the stationary coach, couldn't hit at least one of the four Indians who were cavorting on foot and horseback less than forty yards away. Maybe he missed on purpose, Charvein thought, and only shot one of the horses to make it appear he was trying.

He pushed this thought to the back of his mind, resolving to watch Breem even closer than before. He went to the coach and looked in the open door. "How's the patient?"

"Sleeping," Satterfield said. "Good thing. He was in a lot of pain. But the whiskey put him out for now. Probably needs a doctor to set that broken arm."

He and Charvein looked blankly at each other. "You know of a doc within a hundred miles of here?" Satterfield asked.

"Neither of us is from Norton's Landing. I don't know," Charvein said.

Satterfield rubbed a hand over his thick mustache. "Gotta be somebody in a settlement like that who's had experience treating gunshot wounds." He nodded at the man. "He won't be inspecting any more mines this trip. Maybe we can figure out a way to get him back before that wound mortifies."

"If you come up with an idea, let me know," Charvein said. "Meanwhile, let's get the team hitched if we want to make the Carbuncle mine before dark." He pointed at Breem. "After we're clear, trail the odd horse on behind the coach."

The men shortened up the traces and managed to reharness the remaining four-horse team. "Okay, let's get this coach outa here!" Charvein climbed to the driver's seat. "Breem, you and Satterfield push when I give the word."

Sandoval went to help and the three men took up positions behind the Concord

Charvein took the long coach whip out of its socket and kicked off the brake. "Hyah!" He popped the whip over the ears of the team and the horses leaned into their breast bands. "Giddap! Hyah!" The whip popped like a gunshot and the horses strained, hooves digging into the loose soil and rocks.

The left front wheel sucked up from the submerged gravel. The coach rolled up onto solid rock. Muscles bunched on the big draft horses and their digging hooves finally got purchase. They continued scrabbling until the coach was on level ground above the lip of the rise.

"Whoa!" Charvein hauled up on the reins, set the foot brake and stepped down.

Breem brought up the wheeler to tie him off to the back of the coach.

Charvein reached for one of the hanging canteens, uncorked it and took a long swig. "Go ahead and get in," He called to Satterfield. "Be there in a minute." He motioned Sandoval away from the coach and handed him the canteen. "Gotta ask you something," he began, glancing back to be sure they were out of earshot. "Did you dig that gold out of the church ruins after Lucy and I left Lodestar?"

Sandoval regarded him with hooded, expressionless eyes. "Strange you should ask. I was going to put the very same question to you." He went on to relate the conversation he'd overheard in the Virginia City saloon between Stripe Morgan and his boss, Ezra Pitney, when the two men had discussed scouring the church rubble, but coming up empty. "I thought maybe you doubled back and took that gold after I left Lodestar a day or so later," he concluded.

"I'll be damned!" Charvein looked away at the coach that stood waiting in the hot sun. "That explains why Polecat Morgan came after me." He quickly told of his harrowing brush with death at the hands of Pitney's bodyguard aboard the steamboat.

Sandoval whistled softly. "I saw the partly burned *Gila* land at Yuma earlier in the week. Sheriff came aboard and arrested Stripe Morgan."

"Thank God he's out of the way for a while, then," Charvein said. "When he was about to hang me with my saddle, I pretended to know where the gold was. Had to buy time for an escape. Yet nobody seems to know who really *did* take it." He paused. "It seems odd," he said, thoughtfully, "I saw those bell clappers and knew they were made of gold. What I didn't see was the other ingots and the cross you said you made of the remaining metal."

"I swear on my dead wife's grave, I told you the truth," Sandoval insisted urgently, making a sign of the cross over his heart. "It was there before we blasted the church. And I didn't touch it after you left. I waited only a day and decided I could travel with a wounded arm if I took it easy. So I packed up and left. Rode a long, roundabout way to Virginia City and went into hiding with a friend."

"I believe you," Charvein said. "But that still leaves the mystery." He stopped talking when Breem came walking toward them.

"You ready to get underway?" the guard asked, looking grim.

"Yeah." Charvein took a step toward the coach and heard a sudden scuffle behind him. He whirled and saw Breem had snatched Sandoval's pistol from its holster and backed off a step, holding two pistols on Sandoval.

"What's this?" Charvein cried. "You gone crazy?"

Sandoval looked stunned, still holding the Colt Lightning at his side.

"Drop that rifle!" Breem snapped. "I'm taking you into custody for murder."

"Who the hell *are* you, anyway?"

"A bounty hunter. Wanted posters with your picture and description are plastered all over the Territory. There's a $5,000 reward on your head and I aim to collect it."

CHAPTER 23

"You're outta your mind," Charvein said. "Put that gun down."

"Drop your rifle," Breem repeated, trying to cover both men at once.

Sandoval carefully placed the Colt Lightning on the ground and held his hands out to his sides.

Charvein's heart was racing, but he was wary of making any sudden moves. Breem appeared in deadly earnest.

"You got the wrong man," Charvein said. "I know Carlos Sandoval, and he's not wanted by the law."

Holstering one of the six-guns, Breem reached inside his shirt, pulled out a folded flier and tossed it on the ground at Charvein's feet. "Take a look at that if you don't think I have the right man!"

Charvein picked it up and unfolded the stiff paper. The crude drawing didn't really resemble Sandoval but the write-up did. Charvein knew the story on this and there was no way Breem was going to arrest his old friend.

"Apparently, you haven't been keeping up with the paper on your fugitives," Charvein said disgustedly. "This wanted poster is old and long out of date. Buck Rankin's dead. Since he turned out to be an outlaw himself, the state of Nevada has withdrawn the reward. Sandoval's shooting of his wife was ruled accidental." Enough of this was true that Charvein was able to make it sound convincing. "When's the last time you updated your list of fugitives?" He made it sound as if this were all a big mistake. "Come on. Let's get out of here. We have time to make up."

"You think I'm gonna let $5,000 slip through my fingers on your say-so?" Breem was scornful.

"How you plan to handle all of us at once if we don't agree with you?" Charvein said, nodding toward Satterfield by the coach, who apparently was far enough away that he couldn't hear what was taking place.

"I'll ride this here extra coach horse, and Mr. Sandoval and I'll go back over the hill to pick up his animals and gear. Then we're headin' straight to the marshal's office in Yuma. You can tell Belcher I quit. More important business to tend to."

Charvein caught Sandoval's eye and gave an almost imperceptible nod.

The three men moved toward the stage and Satterfield saw Breem's drawn gun.

"What's going on here?"

Nobody answered him.

"Go get that horse," Breem ordered.

Sandoval yanked loose the leather strap that tethered the extra horse to the back of the stage.

"I'll ride bareback and you lead me over the hill to your place," Breem carefully maneuvered to keep the other three men in front of him. "If either of you want to interfere, you'll wind up in worse shape than that tenderfoot in the coach." He gestured with his gun. "Now, take your pistols and toss 'em into the creek."

Charvein and Satterfield had no choice but to obey, walking down the incline and pitching the weapons into the shallow water.

With two quick bounds, the bow-legged guard nimbly hopped onto the rear wheel hub and leapt onto the big horse's back. He took the long rein and pulled the animal's head around. "Okay, Sandoval, lead on." He kicked the animal in the ribs. With a last look, Sandoval walked away toward the open desert.

Charvein moved cautiously until the coach was between him and the retreating Breem, who was keeping an eye over his shoulder.

Charvein scooted his feet several yards sideways to where Sandoval had laid down the Lightning. He felt for the rifle with his foot, then waited patiently until the horseman, following Sandoval, was a good fifty yards away and just starting up the long slope to the top of the hill. Then he slowly squatted and retrieved his old rifle, standing it up next to him without any further movement.

He counted slowly to ten and then walked back to the coach, pumped a shell into the chamber and laid the barrel of the rifle over the front footrest on the driver's side. The rider was far enough away now that details were indistinct. Taking careful aim through the buckhorn sight, he lined up Breem's back, held his breath for two seconds and squeezed the trigger. The rifle jumped and through the haze of smoke, he saw Breem tumble off the horse.

"By damn, you got him!" Satterfield cried.

"Hope I didn't kill the little bastard," Charvein ran around the coach for a better look. "But violence is the only thing some people understand."

The two men ran toward the fallen guard. Sandoval was crouched by him when they arrived.

"You shot me, you sonofabitch!" Breem spat at them, his eyes blazing. He gripped his right shoulder, blood seeping between his fingers. "I'll have you arrested for interfering with the lawful performance of my duty."

"You won't do a damn thing but lie there and be quiet until we can get you bandaged up," Charvein took Sandoval's pistol from the guard's belt and tossed it to his friend.

Sandoval had already taken both the carbine and the pistol that had fallen when Breem was hit.

"Since you seem to be the best doc on the premises, how about fixing him up," Charvein said to Satterfield. "If it's not too bad, we'll leave him at the mine to recover until he feels up to traveling."

Satterfield moved to comply without comment.

"In fact, we can leave both our wounded men at the Carbuncle and let the mine superintendent take them back to town later."

In twenty minutes, the coach was ready to go, the two wounded passengers inside with Satterfield. Satterfield had managed to bind the shoulder wound and stop the bleeding, but Breem was weak and subdued.

"You saved me," Sandoval said as Charvein climbed to the box and took up the reins. "I didn't know I was still a wanted man until I found a copy of that wanted poster tacked to a fence in Yuma last time I was in town."

"I really don't think you're still wanted by the law. But you'd best lie low anyway until I can check it out with the marshal's office in Virginia City."

"You might be arrested for shooting that bounty hunter."

Charvein shrugged. "Nobody pulls a gun on me and kidnaps my best friend. That handbill he showed said the reward would be paid for you dead or alive. If I ever come to trial for attempted murder, I can always say I was aiming at you so I could collect the reward myself. I can't help it if I'm a poor shot. Anyway, from the looks of that wound, it'll be a good while before he's well enough to file charges. If I'm still anywhere to be found, I'll deal with it then."

"That was a very skillful shot."

"I wasn't aiming for his shoulder," Charvein admitted. "I pulled the barrel slightly off line when I squeezed the trigger. The Providence you believe in so strongly saved me from becoming a killer." He glanced at the black vultures beginning to circle in the pale blue sky. How did they get the message so quickly in this vast desert? From the number of black specks gliding silently overhead, it appeared all the distant kin were gathering to feast upon two freshly killed horses by the creek.

"Another thing," Charvein said. "Somebody tried to rob the stage last night while it was parked at the mine. I didn't get a good look, but think it might've been that little bandy-legged guard. I can't prove anything, but I wouldn't be surprised if he also put those Apaches up to attacking us today so he could get his hands on the strongbox."

"You quitting this job?"

"If all my runs are gonna be like this I will. Haven't been employed long enough to miss it. I'm sure Belcher will fire me anyway, when I report back. Then again, maybe he won't. We'll see. Meanwhile, can you meet me in Norton's Landing four or five days from now? If you get there before I do, put up your animals at the livery and wait for me.

"You have plans?" the dark, slender man squinted up at him in the sunlight.

"I think we need to work together to find out who took Pitney's gold. Neither of us is going to be safe until we do. And it likely beats prospecting."

"Our destinies seem to intertwine." Sandoval nodded solemnly, stepping back from the coach. *"Vaya con Dios!"*

Charvein popped the lines over the team and the coach rolled away, wheels churning up the powdery dust.

Chapter 24

With a great sense of relief, Stripe Morgan came down the steps of the Yuma County courthouse and breathed the fresh, free air of the desert autumn. The coal oil and cigar smoke odor of the inside air could be quickly exhausted from his lungs, but the memory of his ordeal not so quickly forgotten. Only by the merest chance had he escaped being charged with arson, or burglary or attempted murder. He had not even been fined. It was all just an unfortunate accident, so he let on to the sheriff during more than a day of questioning. Morgan had indignantly insisted he was only defending his property against a burglar, and had wound up paying the price by the loss of his belongings and several burns to his person.

As he started down the street, on the lookout for a saloon to celebrate, his movements were somewhat restricted by the various plasters and bandages under his new clothes that covered patches of burned skin.

Twenty minutes later he found an adobe saloon with a patio shaded by the gray-green leaves of several paloverde trees. He leaned back in a wooden chair, sipping a beer, the top of his shirt open to admit a cooling breeze against his raw skin.

Only an hour before he'd been a prisoner in the county jail. Then the sheriff had unlocked and swung open his cell door. "You're free to go," he said with no preliminaries, handing over Morgan's gunbelt, billfold and money confiscated the day before.

Morgan grabbed his belongings and headed for the door, wanting to ask for details of his release. But, long ago, he'd learned never to look a gift horse in the mouth. Now, out of detention, he thought he knew why he'd been freed—lack of evidence, no witnesses. He'd sent Claudine out of the room before the fight with Charvein. The lamp had been broken, starting the fire. He and Charvein had fired at each other, both missing. Then Charvein had gone over the side. The small cabin had been destroyed and flames burned through the overhead before the crew could extinguish the blaze with sand, buckets of water and wet blankets.

Knowing it could only hurt his case, Morgan had not mentioned either Claudine or Selinger. He was thankful the two actors had vanished in the confusion of the fire and apparently departed quickly after the boat landed at Yuma the next day.

When questioned by police, Morgan told them someone had slipped into his unlocked cabin and waylaid him when he came in. Did he know his assailant? No. Did he know why the man was in his cabin? No, but assumed he'd surprised the intruder in the act of ransacking the cabin for valuables. A fight ensued and each man fired a shot. During the struggle, the lamp was shattered, setting the cabin ablaze. The burglar broke down the outside cabin door and escaped.

The purser and first mate had checked all the cabins on the boat, taking a roll call of passengers. All were accounted for, except a man named Marc Charvein who'd occupied cabin twelve. He was nowhere to be found. Strangely, the lock on his cabin door was broken. Only a few personal items were found, but nothing that could tell them anything about the missing man. The purser described this Marc Charvein and said he'd come aboard carrying a saddle, but none was found in his cabin. The charred saddle found in Morgan's room he quickly claimed as his own.

One of the deckhands thought someone jumped or fell overboard on the starboard side just before he heard shouts of fire. But he couldn't be sure. Someone on the upper deck might have thrown something over the side. The sheriff concluded the burglar had jumped and either escaped, or his body would eventually wash up somewhere along the river.

No witnesses. Morgan smiled grimly, taking another sip of his beer. And only his word concerning the incident. However doubtful the sheriff and the boat captain were about his tale, there were no witnesses to either confirm or deny his story, so the matter was dropped, leaving the owners of the *Gila* to file a claim for insurance and repairs.

With any luck, word of this wouldn't get back to Ezra Pitney.

Leisurely finishing the beer, he rose to find a store and replace his torn and blackened clothing. He still had money for traveling expenses, and he had his gun. What else was needed? He'd allow himself a few days to rest and recuperate, then take to the trail of the man who'd caused all this trouble. Instinct told him Charvein still lived and was somewhere upriver. Next time he got the slippery thief in his clutches, he wouldn't play any games making him talk; he'd devise some exquisite torture that would force out the truth quickly. After all, when Charvein thought he was about to be strangled, he'd admitted guilt and was on the verge of offering to lead Morgan to the gold. But then all hell broke loose.

CHAPTER 25

Lucinda Barkley was enjoying herself immensely.

The day was warm and sunny with a nice westerly breeze. And she could relax because she sensed her teenage Mexican boatman was nearly in awe of her—a wealthy, good-looking white woman who'd hired him to transport her up the Colorado River.

As the sun tipped the eastern horizon, she looked back to see they were already a half-mile northwest of the village on the Sea of Cortez and nearly out of sight of the steamship she'd just left. It was a pleasant surprise to see the estuary was at least a mile wide with one or two islands in it. This unusual width extended upstream as far as she could see to the next bend in the distance.

She'd been fearful the young boatman would not be able to row or sail, or tow the boat against the current. But she needn't have worried. The tide was coming in, nullifying the south-bound current, a southwesterly breeze had sprung up with the heat of the morning sun, and the homemade cotton sail bellied out to starboard as Victorio had the boat sailing on a broad reach, nearly directly upstream.

Even though the boat was carving a bow wave and they were making good time now, she knew this wouldn't last. Victorio had told her the river eventually narrowed and the current grew stronger several miles upstream. But for now, she sat with her back against her two leather bags in the middle of the 17-foot boat and inhaled the fresh smell of the desert. "We're making good time, Victorio," she said. Maybe she could draw him into conversation. It would be a distraction from her thoughts that Sam Stonehouse was likely on her trail.

"*Si, señora.*"

"I'm not a *señora*. I'm a *señorita,*" she corrected him.

"*Pardon.*"

The young man stood in the stern, feet braced wide, gripping the long tiller to keep the heeling boat on course as the breeze freshened. Because of the overnight chill and his modesty before this woman, he was wearing long trousers, going to tatters above the ankles, and a long-sleeved white shirt patterned with some sort of green floral and fish design. She wondered if it was his Sunday shirt.

He had not asked her how far she wanted to go on this up-river tour. She'd mentioned only a day excursion, withholding the information that she wanted to go all the way to Yuma, some fifty miles north. She'd spring it on him later when the river narrowed and became swifter so he'd have to row or tow the boat in the slack water near the bank. She noted he kept a pair of corded sandals under the stern seat to protect his feet ashore.

"Were you named after the great Apache chief, Victorio?" she inquired.

"No, *señorita*. My people have been enemies of the Apache for many years. And I do not think Victorio was his Apache name."

Lucy nodded. "You're right. Probably something the whites invented because they couldn't pronounce his real name."

If this had not been a necessary trip, Lucy would have enjoyed the outing even more. As it was, she took in the scenery of this wild country with the thought constantly in the back of her mind of what she would do when she reached Yuma. But reaching and crossing the border was her first goal. What she could see from the low aspect of the boat was mostly creosote bush, yucca with its translucent needles, the spiky arms of saguaro cactus reaching toward the sky. Few flowers were in evidence this time of year. There was a low range of hills miles to the west, apparently the tailbone of the Rocky Mountains extending down into the Baja peninsula—all in all, a stark, but strangely beautiful, landscape.

The river began to narrow and made several sharp bends within a five-mile stretch, causing an adverse headwind when the boat was pointed west. Three times he had to unlimber the oars and row upstream, hugging the slack water along the bank until the river curved again and they picked up a fair breeze. The river here was too narrow and too swift to make progress by attempting to tack a zig-zag course against the wind. He took advantage of the difficulty of navigation every couple of hours by letting the current push them to the bank or onto a sandbar. Then he tied off the bow to the handiest driftwood and they stepped ashore to stretch their legs and disappear behind clumps of bushes to urinate.

Finally, she judged it was nearly noon by the overhead position of the sun and her own rumbling stomach. In her excitement to leave before dawn, she'd neglected to eat. But the night before she'd had the foresight to steal as much hard bread and dried beef strips from the galley as she could hide under her shawl. And she had two large canteens full of fresh water.

How far had they come? The steady wind had been about ten miles per hour out of the southwest since shortly after sunrise. She judged the boat had averaged maybe three miles an hour, most of it directly upstream. As the river bent more westerly, the wind had nearly headed them, and Victorio had resorted to short tacks, and finally to oars. Even so, Lucy guessed they had gained at least eighteen miles upriver.

"Would you like something to eat, Victorio?" she asked after a long silence, reaching into her smaller bag for a loaf of hard bread.

"*Gracias,* but I brought some tortillas and beans, which I intended to share with you," he said, almost shyly. "Would you like to stop and eat ashore?"

"Not unless you're tired," she said. "I'd rather keep going."

"Then we will eat while we sail. I can fish all day and not be tired."

"Is this better than fishing?" she asked.

"*Si.* Much better," he smiled. "Maybe I will do this one week when the ships come in, and then fish when the ships are not in port."

"A good idea. I'm sure the passengers would like to see the river and the desert after being cooped up on the ships for weeks from California."

Lucy tore off a piece of bread and chewed it with a strip of jerky. Most of the food in the galley was fresh and there was little she could confiscate that wouldn't spoil.

Victorio accepted—out of courtesy, she felt sure—a piece of hard bread. And she relished a tortilla he offered wrapped around red beans.

The afternoon passed swiftly for her and before long, the sun was sliding down the western sky toward the spiny row of distant mountains. She noted him glancing that way with a look of concern.

Finally, he said, "It is nearly time to start back. Even with the current, it will be midnight before we arrive at the village. But the moon will be bright to guide us."

"How far have we come?"

"Hmmm . . . I think maybe twenty-five miles."

"Victorio, I have not been completely honest with you," she said. "I will make you the richest young man in the village if you'll do me a favor."

"Yes?" His brow knitted with an intense seriousness that nearly made her laugh.

"I really want to go all the way north to Yuma. If you will continue on, I will pay you well. We are about halfway now."

He didn't reply at once, but gazed around at the barren, lonely landscape, the silent desert, with long shadows stretching out from the saguaros. *"Si,"* he said finally. "I will do it. I must make a bed in the bottom of the boat for you to sleep during the night."

"I can manage. Will you be able to stay awake and sail?"

"We are coming to a part of the river where I cannot sail. I must use the oars."

A late-afternoon breeze stiffened, heeling the boat to starboard. He stopped talking and loosened the secured mainsheet, spilling air from the sail and allowing the boat to right itself.

"We still have a good breeze and it might last until after dark," he said, "so if we are to go that far, I must use all the wind I can while it blows."

"Yes."

"Tell me, *señorita,*" he said, "why is it that you did not wait for the steamboat to take you to Yuma?"

"I can't tell you that, Victorio. It is personal, but I have a good reason."

Since he seemed a little hesitant, she sought to reassure him of the reward that awaited his effort. She got to her knees and unlocked the small padlock on the larger leather bag to retrieve a tiny pouch of gold dust.

Apparently, he was watching her and not paying attention to his sailing because suddenly the boat veered and he muttered something as he quickly corrected his course with the tiller.

Lucy was thrown off balance and the heavy gold cross slid out of the open bag, thudding into the bottom of the boat. The long rays of sun caught the metal, making it glow.

"*Santa Maria!*" he marveled, gazing at it.

She hadn't intended for him to find out what she carried, but it was too late now. Gold in this amount could make even the most respectful native boy suddenly become greedy. But she carried her loaded pistol in her skirt pocket, just in case.

Lucy muscled up the cross with both hands, and propped it against the thwart. "I didn't mean for you to see this, Victorio, but it's what I must take to Yuma. And I didn't trust some of the people on the steamer," she lied. But it was only a partial lie. Stonehouse would be on the next steamer as well; it was him she feared.

"That is most beautiful," he made the sign of the cross on himself. "Did it come from a church?"

"I didn't steal if from a church, if that's what you mean." She'd never looked upon it as an object of veneration, until now. "A hermit made this cross for himself and kept it in a church until the building was destroyed. He was not a craftsman, so the workmanship is crude."

"He worked from his heart, not from his skill," the young man said. "We have many such artists in Mexico."

She slipped out a ten-dollar gold piece and handed it to him. "This is for now," she said. "There will be another eagle for you when we reach Yuma."

He accepted and pocketed it, smiling.

Twilight deepened while he kept the boat angling across the current with the dying breeze.

"If you need to rest, tie off to the bank," she said.

"Often I have fished all night, *señorita*. So I can keep the boat moving while you sleep." He glanced around at the gathering dusk. "Many predators come out at night in the *gran desierto*," he said.

She had the feeling he was not comfortable with the unseen dangers of desert darkness.

Wrestling the gold cross back into the leather bag, she snapped the padlock closed on it. The bag made a hard mattress, but she leaned back against it, sliding a hand into her front skirt pocket to close around the butt of her .38.

Darkness crept over the river and stars appeared. A soft swishing and gurgling of water past the hull lulled her into a doze. She dreamed of her luxurious bath in the San Francisco hotel.

CHAPTER 26

"Helluva trip for your first time out," Belcher walked around the stagecoach and inspected the bullet holes in the thin wood.

"I delivered every payroll to the mines on time," Charvein said with an upbeat tone.

Belcher opened the door of the coach. "Blood all over the seats and floor. And you lost one of the horses, too."

"You had to have been there." Satterfield, the geologist, stood under the awning in front of the Wells Fargo office in Norton's Landing. "We were damned lucky." He and Charvein exchanged glances.

"The shotgun guard and the other passenger both wounded," Belcher continued. "That's not good for business. Turns off investors."

Charvein was irritated at Belcher's tone.

"Investors don't care what happens out here as long as they get a good return on their money. And I haven't heard you've lost any ore shipments."

"That's not the point. It's bad publicity."

Charvein shrugged, expecting to be fired.

"I'll have to send a spring wagon to the Carbuncle mine to pick up Bud Archer and Breem. Hope their wounds haven't mortified."

"Might have to get a few of the cavalry to escort us on these runs," Charvein said.

"What cavalry?" Belcher asked. "Not but a handful of soldiers still stationed across the river at Fort Yuma. The commander there can't spare anybody."

"Guess those bronco Apaches know they've got free rein, then," Charvein said.

"They jumped us from cover of the trees by the creek," Satterfield added. "We did the best we could."

Belcher didn't reply, but stood back with hands on his hips and surveyed the damaged coach as if calculating what it would cost to replace the horse and clean up the Concord.

Anticipating Belcher's next words, Charvein said, "Frankly, I don't blame your last driver for quitting, if he went through what we did. Anybody hankering for that kind of action could join the cavalry."

"For a lot less pay," Belcher said. "And speaking of pay, I'm increasing your salary. But try not to destroy so much company property next time, will ya?" He grinned and shook his head.

Charvein breathed easier. He still had a job. "When's my next run?"

"About a week."

"The stage again?"

"No. You'll have a couple o' tough mules and a freight wagon. If you can handle a six-horse hitch, you can damn sure deal with a span of stubborn mules."

"I'll be out of town a few days," Charvein said.

"Report back to me at the warehouse on . . . let's see . . . October 6. By the way, I pay by the trip, so come on over to the office. I won't deduct that horse from your wages."

"Be right there." Charvein turned aside and extended his hand to Satterfield. "Thanks for all your help. I'd take two or three like you backing me in any kind of scuffle."

"My pleasure," the geologist rubbed his thick gray mustache. "Gonna seem mighty dull in Phoenix compared to this."

"You headed back today?"

Satterfield nodded. "Riverboat to Yuma, then on the east-bound Southern Pacific to Tucson. Couple days at my sister's there, and then home to Phoenix."

They shook hands. "By the way," Satterfield said, "in case that bounty hunter makes it, you can count on me not to be available for any inquest."

Charvein smiled grimly. "Thanks."

He collected his pay in cash from Belcher, signed the receipt and headed for the hotel. It would be good to have a bed to sleep in after several days on the mine circuit.

As he dipped the pen in the inkwell to sign the register at the desk, someone touched his elbow. A Mexican in a straw hat. "I have something for you, *señor*," said a heavily accented voice.

Charvein put down the pen and turned away with Sandoval. They stepped outside under the porch roof.

"When did you get here?"

"Couple hours ago. Stayed out of sight until you were free. I'm nervous in towns."

"Maybe in Virginia City, but why here?"

Sandoval looked around and then carefully produced the wanted poster. "Tore that off a fence in Yuma."

"Hmm . . . yeah, I forgot. It's best to be cautious. Especially since that damned Breem tried to arrest you. If he had one of those fliers, there could be others out there floating around—and ambitious men looking to collect the reward."

"Yes," he nodded. "I don't want to be surprised again. Next time it might not turn out so well." He glanced around. The late-afternoon street was nearly deserted. "Is that guard going to live?"

"I don't know. Belcher is sending a wagon up to the mine to fetch him and Bud Archer back here. That'll make nearly a week since both of them were shot, and nobody with any medical skill to tend them."

"I hate to stay on the run for the rest of my life," Sandoval said thoughtfully. "But there is no statute of limitations on murder."

"Maybe you should turn yourself in and go to trial to settle this once and for all," Charvein suggested. "After all, killing your wife *was* an accident."

"With a white jury, who will believe that? The only two witnesses are dead, including Buck Rankin. Since I wounded Rankin, I would be found guilty of shooting a lawman in addition to killing my wife. Men shoot their wives every day when they catch them in the act of being unfaithful. I'd be found guilty and hanged. It would also get very complicated because Lucy shot and killed Rankin when he was about to put a knife into you. As of now, nobody but us three know for sure what happened to him." He shook his head. "No, it's better that all this be left alone. No surrender, no courts, no explanation. God alone will judge us all."

"You're right. Let dead bodies lie," Charvein said. "You have your animals stabled?"

"Yes."

"I thought we'd go down to Yuma and nose around."

"You think Polecat Morgan is still in the county jail?" Sandoval asked.

"That's one thing I want to find out. I'll breathe easier if I know he's behind bars. Mind leaving your animals at the livery while we poke around Yuma and make a few inquiries?"

Sandoval shrugged. "Fine. I don't know what you expect to find there."

"Yuma's about the only civilized town in this part of the country, except for these little river ports," Charvein said. "News gets around. Travelers come and go. It's not only local stuff. Whoever took Pitney's gold probably didn't hang around

Virginia City with it."

"But there are many better places the thief could go to spend it."

"True enough," Charvein said. "But I haven't yet been to Yuma. A town attracts people. I want to see what's there."

"Then we will go," Sandoval said. "When?"

"I don't have a horse. Let's get a good night's sleep and catch the riverboat down in the morning. The *Pima* is offloading at the landing now, and will start south at daylight. It'll take most of the day to get there."

"I have not slept in a bed for weeks," Sandoval eyed the front door of the hotel. "It will seem strange."

"Not any stranger than the life we've been living the past few months."

"Yes." He regarded Charvein with expressionless, hooded eyes. "I have made up for the peaceful time in Lodestar."

Sandoval had stowed his rock hammer and camp gear in a pack with his animals at the livery stable and carried no luggage with him on the boat. When he stepped aboard the next morning, he wore a woven poncho over his cotton shirt and canvas pants, carried his open top Colt conversion in a belt holster, cleaned and loaded. "I will not be caught off guard again," he answered when Charvein remarked about the care his friend was taking of his sidearm.

"I'm traveling light, too," Charvein patted his Merwin Hulbert. He had attached the longer, six-inch barrel to the .32. And he carried no extra clothing—only extra cartridges and several one- and five-dollar gold pieces.

They purchased one-way tickets, deck passage.

The *Pima* pilot tapped the bell. The paddlewheel began to slap the water and the sternwheeler swung out into the current and headed downstream.

It was a beautiful, peaceful morning, the kind of day that made a man glad to be alive. From the vantage of the boiler deck, they watched the brown river slide past. The empty desert on both sides looked as if no human had ever been there, but this area had a long history of Indian settlement.

Charvein could appreciate why Sandoval looked back with some nostalgia on four years spent as a hermit in the ghost town of Lodestar. But, by rescuing Charvein out of a nocturnal dust storm, Sandoval had changed both their lives forever.

CHAPTER 27

The *Pima* made a smooth run with no mechanical trouble and the pilots skillfully avoided grounding the steamer on shifting sand bars. The boat nosed into the landing at Yuma next to the moored *Mojave* just before six that evening.

"There's a good eating place in the train depot," Sandoval said. "It's one of those Harvey House restaurants. I ate there last time I was in town."

"Your word's good enough for me. Let's go."

They fell into step and headed for the depot they could see two blocks ahead of them.

"I hear a train whistle," Charvein said.

"The night train to Los Angeles," Sandoval replied. "I checked the schedule when I was thinking of going there. But decided to lose myself in the desert instead of the City of Angels."

"You realize how crazy that sounds?"

"What?"

"The night train to Los Angeles. The fact that anyone could travel that far, that fast, still amazes me. It took us all day today to travel fifty miles by steamboat."

"Yeah, that passenger train will be on the coast by mid-morning."

"The world is changing," Charvein said. "I was a railroad detective a few years ago, so I'm familiar with trains, but I didn't ride them all that much. The idea of really fast travel still puts my mind in a whirl. I'm still geared to the speed of the horse, or six of them, pulling that stagecoach."

"I've let the world go by, too," Sandoval nodded. "The solitude and pace of the desert suits me."

They entered the big waiting room and headed for the dining area walled off at one end. A 4-4-0 locomotive, bell clanging, chugged past the windows and squealed to a stop in a blast of steam. The coaches were positioned at the platform. Passengers began to debark.

Wood smoke drifted into the room, mingling with the aroma of frying meat from the kitchen.

They sat down and ordered supper from an attractive young lady in a black frock covered with a neck-high, starched white apron. All the waitresses were dressed alike.

They'd barely beat the rush of passengers from the train who swarmed into the dining room and filled the benches at long tables. The waitresses began taking orders as fast as they could write.

"Harvey House restaurants pride themselves on fast service," Sandoval said. "They claim they can serve a good meal to a whole trainload of passengers and have them back aboard the train in forty-five minutes."

"Amazing. Like I said, the whole world seems to be in a big rush these days."

The room was buzzing with conversation.

"Marc Charvein!"

Startled, Charvein turned toward the woman's voice.

Ten feet away stood Lucinda Barkley.

"Lucy?"

"Yes. Oh, I'm glad to see you!"

Charvein stood and she rushed into his arms.

He hugged her, feeling how thin she was since they'd last traveled together.

"And Carlos Sandoval!" she turned and gave him a hug as well. "My two dearest friends in the whole world."

"What in God's name are you doing here?" Charvein asked. "Come, sit down." He pulled out a chair for her. She was dressed in a blouse and riding skirt and boots and was nearly as dark as Sandoval.

"I was going to ask you the same thing," she said. "What a stroke of luck finding you two here."

Charvein and Sandoval quickly briefed her on their activities since the Lodestar adventure and after Charvein had dropped her off at her parents' home in Carson City. "Had a few other adventures, but I'll fill you in later," he omitted the wild clash with Polecat Morgan and the stagecoach attack.

"I've just been prospecting," Sandoval said, "until I can find something better to do."

Charvein thought she looked upbeat and happy, smiling and laughing, talking excitedly. She didn't bear much resemblance to the pale, disheveled woman he'd escorted back to Carson City, limping from a leg wound. Now, she seemed confident, tanned, a woman of the world who gave no indication of her fascination with the stories of knights and ladies and the French courts of the medieval past. Apparently, her escape into adventurous literature had been replaced by the life of here and now.

"Did your leg wound heal up all right?" he asked.

"Yes, thanks to you. I just have a little scar. It only bothers me when I have to do a lot of walking, especially on hills." Suddenly, she dropped her bright, cheery demeanor.

"Speaking of things from Lodestar, Marc, I need your help," she said quietly, the smile disappearing from her face.

"You in some kind of trouble?"

"Yes." She looked down, twisting the white linen napkin.

Charvein waited for her to continue.

"You're not going to like what I have to say."

"Try me."

Her suntanned face paled slightly. "I . . . we . . . that is . . . Wait, let me start from the beginning by saying that I don't feel a bit sorry about what I did. I feel after all that business at Lodestar when I was kidnapped, nearly died of thirst and hunger, was involved in a gunfight, got shot in the leg and all that. What I mean is, I'll be forever grateful to both of you for saving my life . . ."

"Wait." Charvein put up his hand to stop her. "You saved my life right there at the end or I wouldn't be sitting here now. So I think we're even on that score. Now, take a deep breath, relax and tell us what you want to say."

She paused for several seconds then blurted out, "I stole the gold from the church ruins."

"*Whaat?*" Charvein felt as if someone had kicked him in the stomach. Of all the revelations he was expecting to hear, this was the least likely.

The waitress returned with two steaming plates and set them down. "You can help yourselves to the coffee at the urns over there." She turned to Lucy. "What for you, miss?"

"Roast beef and mashed potatoes, peas," she replied quickly. "I haven't eaten very well for quite a while," she added to Charvein.

Charvein picked up his fork but seemed to have lost his appetite. He set the fork on his plate, his mind barely registering what was going on around him.

She was the one who'd absconded with the gold—Lucy Barkley, of all people! Why hadn't he thought of her before? She'd seemed only interested in getting back home to resume the civilized life she'd lived before being kidnapped as a hostage.

The waitress withdrew.

Charvein and Sandoval looked at each other in wonderment.

189

The interruption by the waitress had given Charvein a chance to rebound from the shock and begin to collect his thoughts. Ignoring his food, he leaned forward on the table and said, "Let me tell you what's happened because of what you did. Ezra Pitney and his bodyguard, Polecat Morgan, went to Lodestar and didn't find the gold where I said it would be."

"I know. I was there when they came, but managed to get away just before they arrived."

"Well, as a result," Charvein went on, "they're convinced I took it, and Pitney sent his man after me. I wasn't on guard, because I had no idea Morgan was coming." He went on to relate the details of the clash on the steamboat.

"I'm sorry about that, but I have my own troubles now," she said rather meekly. "And I need your help. I didn't get that gold alone. I needed help, so I recruited a Virginia City gambler, Sam Stonehouse."

"Ah . . ." Charvein leaned back in his chair. "That explains why I saw you in a buggy with Stonehouse that day in Virginia City, and then couldn't find you anywhere in town afterward."

"We headed out that night, and still just barely beat Pitney and his men. Thank God for a terrific thunderstorm that flooded the playas and stranded them, or they might have seen us and caught us."

Charvein looked at Sandoval who was taking in the conversation as he ate, his dark eyes darting from one to the other.

"Okay, what kind of trouble are you in now?" Charvein asked.

"Sam and I got clean away from Lodestar, then later sold his wagon and mules and lugged the gold to Carson City. With nobody the wiser about our luggage, we caught a train to San Francisco." She paused for a moment and took a sip of water. "We were there just over a week. Sam began to gamble heavily, and to lose our money as fast as somebody could pour gold dust out onto the floor of a saloon. We were living high—the best food, wine, hotel, clothes, but I knew we'd be broke in a short time at that pace. The only reason he didn't want to split up after we made the grab is that by pooling the gold, he thought he could have access to my share, too."

She took a deep breath and continued. "Like many professional gamblers and prospectors, he was hooked, and was convinced he was only one throw of the dice or one card or one spin of the wheel away from making a big strike that would recoup all his losses and then some. And he wasn't satisfied with losing or winning only small amounts at a time." She looked up from twisting her napkin and met his eye. "By the way, in case you think we shared a bed like man and wife, you're totally mistaken." She shrugged. "I don't know why you'd care, but I just wanted you to know. Sam only made love to the goddess of chance."

Charvein finally began to take a few bites of his food. This woman was so unlike the Lucinda Barkley he'd known, she seemed like a stranger. Apparently, the potential was always there, but he never sensed it.

"So how'd you wind up here? Is Sam with you?"

"While Sam was asleep, I checked out with nearly all the gold that was left, including that really heavy cross you cast," she nodded at Sandoval. "I'm guessing Sam's likely on my trail right now."

"Where's the gold?"

"I stored it when I got to town this morning."

"So you came in on the morning train from Los Angeles and are heading east?"

"I didn't arrive here by train. I took a ship from San Francisco down the coast, around Baja and up the Sea of Cortez. The steamer coming down the Colorado to pick up the passengers for Yuma was delayed several days because of fire damage to the *Gila*."

"I know all about that fire," Charvein said grimly. "So how'd you get here?"

"I hired a Mexican fisherman to sail and row me upriver. Took us all day and all night. But I couldn't just sit there and wait for Sam to catch up. We were only twenty miles south of here in the fishing boat when a steamer passed us, heading downstream. That boat will pick up the passengers waiting in the gulf, and any others who've arrived on the next ship as well. And I expect Sam will be among those."

"Sounds as if you got yourself into a mess."

"Marc, I'm scared and I need help. No telling what Sam will do if he catches up with me."

"I don't see how that's really any concern of ours." Charvein was seething at her audacity.

Her face fell. "You know, I was really glad to see you, and not just because I thought you could give me a hand," she said.

Charvein was instantly remorseful, but tried not to show it.

The waitress arrived and departed, leaving Lucy's roast beef dinner. Lucy began to pick at her food, eyes downcast. "I suppose I'll just have to keep on running," she said. "But I'm not sure where."

Charvein looked at Sandoval, who gave a barely perceptible nod of his head.

"Did you ever think about returning the gold, now that you've had your fling?" Charvein asked.

"I need some of it for expenses, but that heavy cross is what's really dragging me down. Believe it or not, I went to a hardware store this morning and bought a small saw with jagged teeth. I plan to cut off the arms of that cross so the smaller pieces will be easier to carry."

"I've lived on that same gold for several years," Sandoval said.

"But, if it wasn't for you, the original robbers, Denson Boyd and his partners who kidnapped me might have gotten it back," she said.

"It's a very mixed-up situation," Sandoval admitted.

"If I try to return the cross to Pitney, he'll have me arrested and put in jail for theft."

"Maybe you could just leave it somewhere and send him an anonymous telegram about where to find it," Charvein suggested. "If Polecat Morgan wasn't in jail, I could get word to him about where it is and tell him I'd somehow gotten it away from the unnamed thief."

"That won't be necessary," a deep voice said from the next table.

A chill went up Charvein's back at the familiar sound of Polecat Morgan, but he didn't turn around.

The sound of a scraping chair and then the broad-shouldered frame of Morgan loomed over their table.

They'd been talking below the rumble of voices in the crowded dining room without taking note of who was seated nearby and behind them.

Polecat Morgan put a hand into his jacket pocket, and Charvein heard the distinct double-click of a cocking hammer. "I have my hand on a .44, so everyone keep your hands on the table."

The bottom seemed to fall out of Charvein's stomach.

"Well, miss, from what I just heard, you're the joker in this deal. I was told a woman was somehow involved in that Lodestar business. Glad to finally meet you. Everyone needs a stroke of luck now and again," Polecat continued. "I just had mine." He spoke evenly, just loud enough for them to hear. "Mr. Pitney will be mighty pleased that I've accomplished my mission." His half-white mustache stretched in an oily smile.

CHAPTER 28

"Sorry to interrupt your dinner, but if you'll all stand up and walk ahead of me out of this dining room, there will be no trouble. The young lady—Lucy, is it?—can lead us to what I'm looking for and I'll take it off your hands." His eyes narrowed in the handsome face. "You won't have to worry about lugging that heavy load around anymore."

"Then what?" Charvein's mind was racing ahead. As the only one at the table who'd clashed with Polecat before, he was confident he could outwit the big man again.

"Then I'll decide what to do with you three."

He acted on the spur of the moment and has no idea what comes next, Charvein thought.

"None of us is wanted by the law," Charvein continued. Close enough to the truth for Polecat, who knew nothing about Sandoval.

"Mr. Pitney will want to see you—maybe administer his own brand of justice."

"You really think you can take us all the way back to Virginia City by yourself?" Charvein sneered. "You don't look to be in real good condition," he noted the edge of a cotton bandage peeking out from Morgan's shirtsleeve. He challenged Polecat with a look.

"By the way, introductions are in order," Charvein said. "I'm sure they'd like to know who's holding a gun on them. This is Mr. Morgan, Ezra Pitney's personal boot licker, known to one and all as 'Polecat' because of the skunk stripe down the middle of his head. In fact, he'd prefer you call him 'skunk'—his favorite nickname."

"You'll pay for that, you son-of-a-bitch!" Morgan hissed under his breath.

"And this is Lucy Barkley and Carlos Sandoval, two good friends of mine."

Lucy and Sandoval stared at Stripe Morgan, stone-faced.

Charvein considered trying to jump Morgan, pin his hand inside his pocket so he couldn't draw the gun. But he quickly dismissed the idea; too many people close by, and some innocent person could be shot since Morgan already had the weapon cocked. Better to get away from this crowded dining room. There would be other opportunities. One on one, with no weapons involved, Charvein doubted he could subdue the younger man who was over six feet and two-hundred pounds of lean muscle. He wondered how many bandages were under Morgan's clothing. *Did my bullet clip him somewhere, or was he just burned?*

Morgan's face was reddening. No more gloating over his upper hand. "The three of you will get up and move away from the table toward the door." His tone was quiet, deadly.

"And if we don't?" Charvein snapped. "Are you going to shoot us where we sit? About ten men would jump you and haul you off to jail." He glanced at Lucy and Sandoval who were staring at him like he'd lost his mind for baiting this man.

"But you'd be dead, and would never see it," Morgan pivoted so the slight bulge in his coat pocket was aimed directly at Charvein's head.

"All right, you have the upper hand for now," Charvein pushed back his chair and stood up slowly, not making any sudden moves. Morgan was literally on a hair trigger and he didn't want to push the man over the edge so he'd carry out his desperate threat.

Lucy and Sandoval rose as well.

Since they hadn't paid for their food, Charvein hoped someone would stop them. But Morgan anticipated this and dropped a five-dollar gold piece on the table as they started toward the door leading out of the dining hall and into the adjacent depot waiting room.

"What'll I do?" Lucy whispered to Charvein.

"Play along and take us to it. We'll figure out something later."

"No talking!" Morgan commanded from behind.

Fifteen or twenty people were milling around in the big room, several in line at the ticket window. The timetable for all east and westbound trains was chalked onto the blackboard over the ticket agent's head.

The far wall of the big room was lined with lockers of different sizes. Lucy took a key from her skirt pocket and approached one of the smaller ones at floor level. She went to one knee, inserted the key in the lock and swung open the wooden door, revealing the metal lining that looked like the inside of an ice box. She dragged out her two leather bags, the smaller one containing clothes and personal items.

"Step back," Morgan ordered, keeping his right hand on his gun in his coat pocket. He gripped the padlocked leather bag with one hand and tugged. "Uh! Heavy. Open it."

She extracted the padlock key and obeyed.

Morgan motioned her out of the way and pushed open the top of the scuffed bag. His eyes widened at the sight. He thrust his left hand inside and touched the gold cross.

Charvein glanced in as well, getting his first look at the object of everyone's desire. Sandoval looked, then averted his eyes. "Wish I'd never molded it," he muttered.

"Lock it up," Morgan said. He turned to Charvein. "You carry it."

"Where?" Charvein hefted the heavy bag and slung it over his back, holding the top with both hands.

"You, Lucy, go to the ticket window and buy four one-way tickets to Los Angeles on this train. Hurry." He handed her three double eagles.

"It's a long way to Virginia City," Charvein again reminded him. "Think you can hang onto us and this bag all that distance while we're changing trains and waiting around depots and eating meals?"

Morgan didn't reply as Lucy stepped to the ticket window and ordered the tickets.

"Coach or Pullman?" the clerk asked.

"Pullman," Morgan said from behind her. "We want one large compartment."

"You're lucky. One was just vacated in car number 30," the clerk stamped the tickets. He glanced at the big wall Regulator. "Better hurry, ma'am," he handed over the tickets and her change. "That train pulls out in ten minutes."

"Let's go." Morgan gestured toward the platform, falling in behind Charvein who was lugging the long leather bag across his back.

The mixed train consisted of a locomotive, tender, an express baggage and mail car, three passengers coaches, two Pullmans and a caboose.

They climbed up the back platform of the last sleeping car, Lucy in the lead and their captor bringing up the rear.

Charvein realized he and Sandoval were still armed. It would have been too obvious for Morgan to take their guns inside the depot or dining room.

But no sooner had the four of them entered the compartment than Morgan closed the door to the passageway behind them and drew the revolver he'd been clutching in his pocket. "I'll take all your weapons," he said. "Draw them slowly and carefully and drop them on the couch."

Charvein pulled his Merwin Hulbert, Sandoval removed his Colt conversion from under his poncho and they placed both sidearms on the couch.

"Now, Missie, I can't imagine that you're not armed," Morgan leered at her. "You can either voluntarily give up any weapons you have, or I'll be forced to disable these two and search you."

Lucy hesitated for a moment, but at a nod from Charvein, she reached into the pocket of her riding skirt and drew out the .38 she'd stolen from her father's house. She placed it on the couch with the others.

"Any knives?"

She shook her head.

"You're sure about that?" Morgan asked, as if anticipating the opportunity to search her.

"I'm sure."

Keeping the drop on them, Morgan quickly scooped the three guns off the couch into a metal trash basket. Without taking his eyes from them and his hand from his gun, he couldn't stop to unload the pistols.

An overhead bunk was folded up into each side of the ceiling. The couches positioned below these would be made up later by the porter into two more bunks.

"Sit down," Morgan ordered. "No—all on one side here, where I can watch you."

They sat, side by side. Morgan, still appearing tense, sat on the edge of the opposite couch, still holding his six-gun. The two leather bags lay on the floor between them.

"Make yourselves comfortable," Morgan said. "We have a long ride."

They heard a blast on the steam whistle from up ahead. Through the streaked glass they could see passengers rushing back in twos and threes from the dining room, a few still wiping their mouths.

A few minutes later, the train jerked into motion and Charvein, with a feeling of helplessness, watched the depot sliding away beyond the window.

The last coaches had nearly cleared the platform when a man dashed out of the depot and sprinted toward the train as it began to accelerate.

Charvein heard Lucy gasp. She was leaning toward the window with a hand to her throat. Her color had blanched beneath her tan.

"You all right?" Charvein gripped her by the shoulders. She seemed to be struggling for breath. "Choking?"

She quickly glanced at Morgan and swallowed a couple of times. "I'm okay," she managed to whisper. She cleared her throat and sat back, still looking as if she'd seen a vision of Satan himself. Her face had the pallor of death.

She caught Charvein's eye and cut her glance quickly toward the window. He looked out, but the train had now passed the platform, and he saw nothing unusual. What had stunned her so—the late arrival running to catch the train? He looked at Stripe Morgan. The big man used one hand to begin picking the three pistols out of the wastebasket. He was paying no attention to his captives.

Sandoval picked up on a nod from Charvein and began talking. "You know how to operate one of those?" he asked Morgan, who was turning the nickel-plated Merwin Hulbert over in one big hand, evidently trying to figure out how to extract the cartridges. He still held his own .44 in the other hand trained on his captives

"I don't reckon I need any instructions from a damned

'breed'," he snapped.

"You look a little faint," Charvein bent over to hug a trembling Lucy. "Lean on me a minute." As his mouth brushed the hair by her temple, he whispered, "What'd you see?"

"Stonehouse!" she breathed into his ear.

CHAPTER 29

The single word froze Charvein. He held her at arm's length, looking intently into her eyes. "You'll feel better directly," he said aloud. But his heart was pounding so hard he was afraid Morgan would notice the thumping shaking his whole body.

He turned to stare casually out the window, trying to assume a bored attitude. But his mind was racing. How did Stonehouse know she was here? The steamer carrying the delayed passengers up from the gulf must have arrived earlier than expected. Professional gamblers had to be observant. If Stonehouse saw Lucy get aboard or tracked her through the ticket agent at the last minute, he'd be persistent enough to search the train from end to end until he found her. This might be a good thing, or at least throw some gravel into the cogs of Morgan's plan.

Except for an emergency, this train wouldn't stop for many miles. He noticed the 4-4-0 high-wheeled locomotive was carrying an extra water tank to allow for ranging farther between water stops. He'd been this way once before four years earlier while working as a railroad detective. He didn't recall any water tanks between Yuma and the other side of the Sand Hills—a barren waste of Sahara-like desert some fifty miles into California. The Arizona desert was a virtual paradise of plants and animals compared to the California side of the river.

While preoccupied with these thoughts, he was staring out the window while the train made a wide curve to the right and he caught sight of the chuffing locomotive and the several cars

201

behind it. Off to the right the squat, ugly buildings of the Yuma Territorial Prison, surrounded by low walls and guard towers, topped a mesa just north of town.

Then the track straightened out and the train slowed and began its descent toward the river.

"Look here, Charvein," Morgan said. "How the hell does this gun open?"

"You're so damned smart, you figure it out," Charvein said, relieved to vent some of his pent-up frustration.

"If that's the way you want it, I can pitch the damned thing off the train, or—better yet—I might just keep it. Some gun dealer would likely pay good money for it."

"Okay." Charvein gave him directions on how to pull the barrel forward and give it a partial turn.

Morgan shoved the .32 under his belt, wincing slightly. "Good. I'll work on it later."

Charvein noticed the painful reaction when the big man jammed the pistol under his belt. He wondered if Morgan was burned or hurt worse than he let on—possibly vulnerable to a coordinated attack by Charvein and Sandoval. But it would have to be a surprise and simultaneous for the two of them to have a chance.

The wooden superstructure of the bridge flicked its triangular pattern slowly past the window.

They cleared the bridge, and from Charvein's memory the terrain was mostly flat and sandy for several miles now. Not that the landscape would have any bearing on what was going to happen inside the coach.

Night was coming on. Even though it was late September, the long, warm day was reluctant to give up, and Charvein could see the orange disk of sun resting atop the distant horizon, casting a golden glow over the desert sand. He wished this was the only gold anywhere around. Pitney's damned stolen treasure had caused no end of trouble. And it wasn't done yet.

He wondered if Lucy's identification of Sam Stonehouse had been correct. After all, the man was sprinting and she'd had only a quick look. Many men resembled one another in general size and build, even to the way they ran. He'd grill her if he could. Perhaps she was so fearful of Stonehouse, she'd begun seeing him everywhere she looked. Any man who faintly resembled her pursuer could send her into a panic. Yet . . . yet, she'd traveled for weeks with Stonehouse. Women were usually more observant than men. Surely, she'd be able to pick him out at a glance unless he was wearing some sort of disguise. Charvein could only assume she was correct.

He looked at the ivory grip of his loaded Merwin Hulbert protruding from Morgan's belt. If he could only get his hands on that gun! But, as long as Morgan held his .44 trained on them, he didn't dare try.

A rap on the door made him jump. No one moved or spoke.

Another sharper rap sounded on the door panel. "Porter!" came the cry from the corridor outside.

"We don't need anything," Morgan called, leveling his gun again and putting a finger to his lips.

"Make up your bunk, sir?" the porter asked.

"Not just yet. Come back later," Morgan said.

"Yessir." Footsteps moved away down the passageway.

Charvein sensed the train beginning to accelerate. The coach rocked gently and he became aware of the steel wheels clicking rhythmically over joints in the rails.

"I'm thirsty," Lucy said. "Is there a dining car on this train?"

"Didn't see one," Morgan said.

"I expect there's a steward up forward who has sandwiches and drinks for sale," Charvein said, recalling his earlier train days.

"You can stand it for now," Morgan growled. "We only barely

got started, so get used to it. This ain't no damned hotel with room service."

Charvein thought Morgan had just begun to realize the task he'd so impulsively taken on. If the man had the capacity of a killer, he could, without being seen, murder them all and dump their bodies off the train during the night. Then, the gold would be his and he could easily lose himself in Los Angeles and never report to his boss.

At the moment, not even the porter knew four people occupied this compartment; he'd heard only one voice.

Then, Charvein thought of the conductor. He would come by sometime or other to punch their tickets, so the four of them couldn't remain completely incognito in here for more than a few hours.

Fifteen minutes dragged by. Morgan seemed to grow more agitated and nervous. He stood and moved about in the confined space, glancing out the window at the deepening twilight.

"Raise that window a little," he finally ordered Charvein. "Get some fresh air in here."

Charvein gripped the handles and tugged the window up several inches, admitting a flow of warm, dry air, tinged with woodsmoke.

Morgan finally put his own .44 back into the side pocket of his coat, withdrew a match and lighted the coal oil lamp in its wall sconce. The flame threw a cheery warm glow over the tiny room.

Charvein wished he could somehow communicate with Sandoval. If they could act at the same instant, they could jump this man and keep him from getting at one of the guns. Lucy's .38 was in one coat pocket and Morgan's own .44 in the other, Sandoval's empty Colt conversion on the bunk and Charvein's loaded .32 under Morgan's belt.

With four of them in the compartment the only floor space between the bunks was restricted by the two leather bags, so that Morgan could not pace about.

Polecat Morgan wouldn't dare sleep in this four-berth compartment with them unless he somehow confined them. Tying up Charvein had not worked aboard the *Gila*.

What would I do if I were in his place? Charvein thought. *I'd lock the three of us inside here and go sleep someplace else. But the window had only a flimsy inside lock and the glass could be broken. An easy escape hatch if the train stopped for water or passengers.* The only viable choice Morgan had, as far as Charvein could see, was to eliminate the three of them, permanently, during the night. It would be impossible for one man to keep all three prisoners on a long journey. It seemed Morgan's only safe way. But how would he do it? Shooting? He could muffle the blasts with a pillow. Poison them with something—coal oil? There didn't seem to be much else handy. And he couldn't force them to drink it. Poison was doubtful. They'd have to be persuaded to eat or drink something tainted with a deadly substance.

Shooting would be most likely, or he could force each of them to jump out the window into this vast desert while the train was traveling at forty or fifty miles an hour. If they survived, they'd be a long time getting help. No—shooting would be Morgan's only safe way. He could throw their bodies out the window and claim he went to another part of the train and came back to find them gone. Even if the train crew bought his story, he'd still have to carry that heavy bag containing the cross.

"Get those bags under that couch," Morgan ordered, aiming a kick at Lucy's small leather bag. "Can't take a step without tripping."

Lucy crouched on the floor and pulled open the big drawer beneath the couch. She put her small valise inside and Sandoval reached to help her lift the big leather pouch.

The bag was draped over the edge of the drawer when a sharp rap sounded on the door. "Tickets, please!" came a voice.

"Gimme your tickets!" Morgan held out his hand.

The three handed over the tickets. He fanned them out like a poker hand and reached for the door, sliding back the bolt. Easing the door inward a foot, he handed out the tickets.

The door was slammed back into Morgan who tripped on the bag and fell back on the couch.

In a flash, the conductor was inside and closed and bolted the door. He was holding a gun.

"Everyone take it easy," he said.

Lucy gasped.

"Yeah, it's your old friend, Sam Stonehouse," the man yanked off the conductor's pillbox cap and flung it aside. "Surprised to see me? You're a slippery little wench, aren't you? Taking off in the middle of the night, leaving me with an empty sack."

Charvein recognized the man he'd last seen driving a buggy in Virginia City with Lucy at his side.

Stonehouse leaned back against the door, the black bore of the revolver covering them all in the crowded room. "I'll have to say, you led me a merry chase."

"How . . ." She cleared her throat and spoke barely louder. "How'd you get here so quick?"

"Huh! I didn't follow the route you took, that's for sure," he loosened the brass buttons of the blue conductor's coat with his free hand.

Charvein was sweating, not entirely from the heat.

"I had to get away," Lucy said. "You were running through our money way too fast."

"Didn't take me long to find out where you'd gone," he said. "Had to threaten the hotel clerk, but all he could say was that heavy sack you took from the safe contained a valuable stone statue as a gift for your aunt in Oregon." He snorted. "Thought you could do better than that. I checked the depot, the liveries and the waterfront. Didn't matter you used a fake name. I expected that, but when I described a good-looking woman with a heavy leather bag, I found out right quick you'd taken a ship bound for the Sea of Cortez with a through ticket to Yuma." He laughed softly. "I just took the train on the chance I could head you off by riding down to Los Angeles, then east to Yuma. But I still nearly missed you. By the time I reached Yuma, I was broke and had to sleep in the depot waiting room last night. Lucky I did or I might not have seen you boarding this train just before it pulled out."

Lucy drooped on the couch like a wet dish rag.

"How'd you get that conductor's uniform?" Charvein asked.

"I'm a gambler and play the odds. In this heat, I didn't figure he'd be wearing a coat and hat any more than necessary. Took a peek into the caboose while the brakeman was out on the back platform and, sure enough, there was the hat and coat hanging on a peg. I grabbed them. Went through the whole train, starting with the day coaches. Didn't find you, so I slipped into this coat and hat and started knocking on compartment doors in the Pullmans. And here you are in the very last car. Pretty simple, really." He smiled grimly. "Can't you even say you're glad to see me?"

Lucy didn't look up.

"I've seen you in Virginia City," Stonehouse went on, looking at Morgan. "You're . . . Skunk . . . something."

"Morgan's the name."

"Yeah. You work for that mine owner."

Stonehouse pointed at Charvein. "And you must be the one Lucy told me about who was with her in Lodestar."

Charvein said nothing. Let the man speculate all he wanted to.

"Who's the 'breed?" He jabbed a thumb toward Sandoval, frowning. "I never forget a face, and I know I haven't seen you before."

Sandoval sat like a carved image.

"Aha!" Stonehouse's face lit up. "Now it's all coming together! You're that mysterious hermit or desert rat I kept reading about—the one nobody seemed to know or had a name for. You're the one who snatched the gold right after the robbers hid it four years ago. You cast those bell clappers and that cross we found." He looked at Sandoval as if the last piece of the puzzle had fallen into place. "You look more Injun than Mex," Stonehouse commented. "Well, now we have the bodyguard of the mine owner, we have the three who survived all that shootout in Lodestar, and we apparently have the gold, lacking the two bell clappers we melted down and spent along the way." He put a foot on the elongated leather bag that was draped over the edge of the open drawer on the floor.

"Lucy, you and I worked hard for this. We're the last owners of *found* gold somebody abandoned. You were my partner and led me to it. Now you've betrayed me and run off with the rest of what we had together. I'm hurt." He feigned a sorrowful look. "What I can't figure out is why you've taken up with these three. They gonna help you spend it? Maybe you hired them to protect you from *me*. What's the story?"

"No honor among thieves," Morgan broke in. "I'm taking this gold cross back to my boss, Ezra Pitney, the original owner. Don't matter how many damned thieves have had it in the meantime."

"You're wrong about that, Skunk." Stonehouse compressed his thin lips in a fine line. "I've got a royal flush and I'm taking the pot." He turned to Lucy. "Unlock that bag. Gotta be sure it ain't a load of rocks—or a statue for your old aunt," he added sarcastically.

She took out her key and released the brass padlock, pulling open the mouth of the bag so he could see inside.

"Ahhh, all this effort wasn't wasted." He reached inside and caressed the rough yellow casting. "Good to see it again. You know, the only bad thing about gold is its weight. Hard to lug around." But the grin on his face belied his complaint.

"I bought a saw and was going to cut it up," Lucy said. "The saw is in there with it."

Charvein looked at her. What did she have in mind? Why give Stonehouse this information? Trying to make it easier for him?

"Take a cut or two with it to see how well it works," Stonehouse ordered.

She dragged out the cross and propped it against the drawer, produced a short handsaw with jagged teeth and began to rake it across one of the arms. Soft as the gold was, she still struggled when the saw began to bite, and slowed her strokes when crumbs of gold started sprinkling down.

"Okay, that'll do," Stonehouse held up a hand. "Won't matter if it's in four or five pieces. I'll have to tote the whole thing anyway. Put it away and gimme that padlock key."

She obeyed.

"Our next regular stop's Indio," Stonehouse said. "I'll be leaving you there—with this." He patted the bag. "Reckon the four of you will be safe enough here until then."

He fished out the conductor's keys from the uniform pocket, then shrugged out of the blue coat, one sleeve at a time, and dropped the garment on the floor. "Meanwhile . . ." he said, pocketing the keys, "whoever might want to come after me is inviting a bullet. And don't think I won't do it just because we're on this train. It'd be self-defense. I'm defending my life and property from mad robbers. I didn't go to all this trouble just to let you take my gold." He reached his free arm behind himself and slid back the bolt on the door. Stepping to one side, he eased it open and took a quick look into the corridor. Then he squatted, grasped the bag by its top handle and dragged it as he backed outside, slamming the door after him.

Charvein heard the keys jingle and then the lock clicked. A scuffling noise receded outside.

Morgan grabbed the door handle but it was locked fast.

Charvein yanked up the window. Pale moonlight showed the flat desert terrain whizzing past at a good fifty miles an hour. "No handholds to climb to the roof," Charvein said.

"He won't be getting off right away, either," Sandoval said.

"I don't really care if he gets away with the gold," Charvein said to Morgan. "You can tell your boss what really happened to it. The three of us can go our own way as soon as we reach Los Angeles." He looked at Lucy. "What about you? You had about enough of all this? You can write this up in your journal. It would make a great book." He was disgusted.

"Oh, Marc, we owe each other our lives. Let's not end it snapping at each other."

"You two can go mooning around later," Morgan said. "I got four guns in my pockets and I have business with that son-of-a-bitch." He backed up a step and slammed his boot heel into the door panel. "Uh!" He bounced back, defeated. He shook himself, took a deep breath and launched himself at the door with a braced shoulder. Nothing. "Damn!" He squared up, seemed to coil like a bucking bronco and slammed his boot heel into the door with all his weight and force behind it. This time they heard something crack. Two more kicks and the center door panel splintered outward.

Charvein took Lucy's grip and swung at the door until the shards of sharp wood were gone. "Big enough now," he said. "I'll go first." He climbed through, half expecting a bullet to slam into him. But Stonehouse was gone. The passageway was empty.

The three others climbed through the broken door.

"Lucy, you know him better than anyone," Charvein said, taking her by the shoulders and looking into her eyes. "Is he a killer, or was that all a bluff?"

He saw fear there. "Money and the thrill of getting it are all he cares about," she said. "He'll kill to keep it."

Chapter 30

Charvein turned to Stripe Morgan. "Give us our guns back. We're not the enemy now."

Morgan hesitated.

Just then the porter came along the passageway. "Hey, what happened to this door?" He looked at the four of them standing beside it. "Is this your room? I'm gonna get the conductor."

Morgan started to grab the slender black man who headed toward the caboose.

"Let him go," Charvein said. "Stonehouse must be up forward. Hurry. Give us our guns. We'll help you. We don't want your damned gold."

Morgan handed Sandoval his Colt and Lucy her .38. Lastly, he pulled out the Merwin Hulbert and gave it to Charvein.

Morgan led the way and they started forward through the train at a fast walk. Out the end door of the Pullman, across the noisy, jolting platforms between cars and through the next Pullman. Then followed three day-coaches. Several passengers were reading by the subdued light of the overhead coal oil lamps. Others had settled down, slouching in their seats to sleep.

They had to find Stonehouse quickly before the conductor caught up and forced some kind of explanation about the broken door.

Sandoval and Lucy paused between cars to reload their weapons. Charvein's still carried its cartridges.

Charvein had no time to think what they'd do when they

caught up with Stonehouse. They arrived at the locked express car that was just behind the tender and the locomotive, but no Stonehouse.

Charvein elbowed past Morgan on the platform and looked through the small glass window in the locked door. The express messenger was seated at a desk shuffling through bills of lading by the light of a small lamp.

Tapping on the window, Charvein motioned for the man to come close. "Did a man with a leather valise come up here in the last few minutes?"

The messenger, looking irritated, leaned forward so he could hear through the window. He shook his head. "Nobody but the crew allowed in here." He turned and went back to his desk.

"He musta dodged into one of those Pullman compartments," Morgan shouted over the roar of wind and clatter of the couplings.

Charvein motioned Sandoval and Lucy back inside the vestibule of the first passenger coach so he could be heard without shouting.

"You worked on trains before," Morgan said, deferring to Charvein. "Where could he be hiding?"

"Try checking the toilets at the end of each car. Also, check under any empty seats." He turned to Sandoval and Lucy. "You two go back and knock on every compartment door in the Pullmans. Anybody answers, tell 'em you're the law and a wanted man is hiding on the train."

The three went back down the aisle, leaving Charvein alone. Where could Stonehouse be? He couldn't have gone far, lugging that heavy bag. He would never have jumped off with the train going fifty miles an hour, and nothing for miles around but a barren desert. Only a very desperate man, or an insane one, would have tried such a thing. He said he was going to get off at Indio, halfway between Yuma and Los Angeles. Charvein estimated they were probably no more than fifty-five or sixty miles out of Yuma. No, he had to be aboard somewhere. But where? Charvein stood still, trying to visualize the structure of the coaches—every alcove, compartment, platform and possible hiding place. He must be close. He'd vanished too quickly to have gone far. The roof. There was quick access up the ladders at each end of the coaches. He went out onto the platform, made sure his gun was safely holstered and began to climb the iron ladder to the roof of the passenger coach.

Thrusting his head up over the car, he looked aft along the train. Moonlight along with the lamplight shining through the narrow slits along the raised catwalk showed no human form. No one could be crouching or lying on the raised ridge of the coaches without being seen. Even the brakeman, if he'd been looking from his cupola in the caboose, could see all the way to the engine.

The swaying of the coach was exaggerated up here. Smoke and cinders blowing back from the stack nearly suffocated him. He climbed back down and paused on the windy, noisy platform, thinking, absently running his fingers through his disheveled hair.

Then he recalled a place where hoboes sometimes caught a ride aboard a passenger train—the rods beneath the cars. Two long truss rods ran longitudinally from end to end under each coach to provide the cars more rigidity.

Only a very desperate man would try to climb beneath the cars with the train moving. Most hoboes who hopped passenger trains this way climbed aboard before the train started, sliding onto the rods, using a board to lie on if they could find one handy. There was just enough space for a man to fit, lying down across the rods only a foot or two above the ground. It was the least desirable place to ride, with wind whipping around, the rocking and jarring of the coach at full speed, sometimes grit being flung up from the ballast along the roadbed.

A three-foot vertical rod used as a handhold was bolted to the outside of each wooden coach. A man who was daring and reasonably athletic could grip this, swing farther alongside the car to grip one of the window sills with his other hand and swing his legs down under the car and slide himself beneath to rest on the truss rods. One slip and he'd fall under the wheels.

Unless Stonehouse was hiding in one of the Pullman compartments, he must be on the rods. They'd looked everywhere else. But what about the bag? No matter how strong and agile a man was, it would be impossible to perform this feat with a heavy bag.

Charvein would have to inspect the undercarriage. He lay down on his belly on the metal platform, gripped the handrails by the steps, scooted forward so that his head and most of the upper half of his body were hanging outboard and down. The ties were flying past his face at a dizzying speed. He had to squirm forward a little more. The roaring, grinding of the wheel flanges against the steel rails, the jerking and banging of the coupling were deafening. Bits of gravel stung his face.

He twisted his head to look back beneath the coach.

Then he saw him, only a few feet away. He was lying across the rods looking forward. Moonlight glinted off the barrel of a pistol and Charvein instantly tried to twist away. The gun flashed and roared, a yellow tongue of flame lancing from the muzzle. The bullet whanged off the metal step and burned across his left cheek. He struggled to pull himself back up onto the platform and out of sight. Another shot roared from beneath the car and stung his left forearm. "Ahh!" He let go of the handrail and rolled onto his back, yanking his own pistol with his right hand. Thumbing back the hammer, he thrust the weapon down alongside the wheel truck and pulled the trigger, trying to shoot parallel to the track. Then he cocked and fired again.

Footsteps thundered inside the car and the door burst open, flooding the platform with light. He saw his left sleeve was bloody.

"What's going on here?" The conductor roared. Morgan was right at his shoulder.

Suddenly, the air brakes locked and everyone was thrown violently forward, Charvein hitting his ribs against the iron stanchions of the railing.

Squealing of steel against steel and sparks sprayed from beneath the wheels. He vaguely heard yelling and bodies and packages falling as the train decelerated in an emergency stop. But the stop seemed to go on for a long time since they were going at least fifty miles an hour and the locomotive was hauling the tender and seven cars. Finally, after more than a hundred yards, the train ground to a halt.

The engineer came running back alongside the train, carrying a lantern.

Charvein struggled to his feet, feeling warm blood soaking his sleeve and running down his cheek.

"You've been shot!" Lucy cried, rushing up.

"Never mind that!" Charvein yelled. "Underneath! Check the rods under this coach!" Charvein yelled. "Stonehouse."

The conductor reached inside the vestibule and brought out a lantern.

Sandoval came up, gun in hand.

The engineer, conductor, Morgan, Charvein, Sandoval and Lucy all climbed down and went cautiously along the moonlit side of the train, the two trainmen flashing the beams of their bull's-eye lanterns.

"He ain't under there now," Morgan said from ten yards away, bending down and looking underneath. He swept the length of the coach with the barrel of his six-gun.

"Maybe one o' my bullets hit him," Charvein said. "Mighta fallen under the wheels."

They reached the caboose and started forward along the dark side of the train away from the moonlight. No sign of Stonehouse, dead or otherwise. Beams of the bull's-eye lanterns darted back and forth, cutting the dark.

"There!" Morgan yelled and swung toward movement in the deep shadow. Two guns roared simultaneously.

Morgan jerked back and fell.

Charvein also fired at the dim figure. But Stonehouse was already on his knees, slumping against the side of the Pullman and then to the ground.

"Dead center," Sandoval checked Stripe Morgan in the light of the engineer's lantern. A red stain was spreading on his shirt-front.

Crouching, Charvein ran forward to the downed figure of Stonehouse and kicked the gun from his hand. But there was no need. He would never fire it again. The gambler's head lay against one of the steel rails as if he were using it for a pillow.

Ten minutes later the two bodies were laid out on the floor of the express car, with the doors locked against the eyes of any curious passengers.

"Nearest law is at Indio," the conductor said, checking his pocket watch. "But we'll stop for water at Salton Station, in fifty-six minutes." He turned to the engineer. "You can get underway, Jim."

"Two robbers had a falling-out and shot each other," Charvein commented for the record. He gripped his forearm in a vain attempt to stop the oozing blood.

The conductor passed a bottle of whisky to Sandoval. Charvein winced as his friend sloshed alcohol on the arm wound where Stonehouse's bullet had cut a shallow groove across the top of the muscle. Sandoval then hacked off the bloody shirtsleeve.

The conductor was inspecting the body of Stonehouse. "Don't see any other wounds. Bullet got him right in the forehead."

"My two shots must've missed," Charvein said. "Reckon when the train slowed enough, he rolled out of his hiding place and hid in the shadows."

He felt a bit stunned by his wounds, loss of blood and the sudden turn of events. He could hardly focus on the bodies lying there. "Two lives cut short for nothing," he said, holding out his arm for Sandoval to finish knotting strips of a towel as a makeshift bandage.

"This man had a heavy leather bag he stole from me," Lucy said. "Where is it?"

They all looked at one another.

"Did anybody see it?" the conductor asked.

Nobody spoke. The locomotive panted softly in the silence.

"It has to be on this train," she said.

"He could have thrown it off a mile or so back, figuring to come back after it."

"Don't think so," Charvein said. "He made it pretty clear he was going to get off in Indio with that bag."

The conductor heaved a sigh. "Well, it'll put us behind schedule, but get a couple more lanterns and we'll search up and down both sides of the train, and we'll even back up a quarter-mile to see if it was dropped back there when the air brakes took hold and jolted everything."

The bag was not found, and Lucy, Charvein and Sandoval went back to their compartment. The locomotive spun its big drivers, gained traction, and chugged northwest into the California night.

"I can't believe, after all we've been through, that the gold cross has been lost," Lucy lamented, slumping down on the couch.

"It's misplaced, not lost," Charvein assured her. "It'll show up somewhere. It didn't just vanish without a trace."

And he turned out to be right.

An hour later, while the train was halted at the water tower at Salton Station, the young fireman, pulling down chunks of split cordwood, found the heavy bag, folded and tucked down under the piled wood near the rear of the tender. He couldn't open it because of the brass padlock, but called the conductor who brought the three forward to the locomotive cab.

"That's it," Lucy said. "Thank God!"

"Better thank my fireman," the conductor said. "He found it."

Lucy hugged the young man, to his consternation and embarrassment,

They went back to their compartment where the porter had made up their bunks. They stashed the bag and turned in to exhausted sleep.

Charvein, hurting from his arm wound and the bullet burn across his cheek, tossed and turned and finally slept, but was troubled by strange dreams.

The next morning they were held at the Los Angeles depot for the county police to show up and take their statements about the two dead men.

The bodies were removed to the morgue. Then the police questioned and dismissed members of the train crew.

Charvein, Lucy and Sandoval had time before they reached the city to make sure their stories coincided. Since both victims had claimed to be from Virginia City, Nevada, Charvein told the police the pair might have been working together to plan and carry out the robbery. Speaking for the three of them, Charvein also said they didn't know anything about next-of-kin to be notified. Perhaps the dead men were carrying some kind of identification.

The police were curious why a woman and two men, who claimed to be her bodyguards, were carrying such a large cross made of solid gold.

"It was discovered by a padre beneath the floor of a Mexican church near the Sea of Cortez," Lucy lied. "Father Rosario knows me well and asked, since I was coming back to this country, if I would take it to one of the Franciscan missions near Los Angeles for him. He promised it to a priest there who's raising money for the restoration of one of the original missions. Earthquake damage, you know."

"Which mission?"

"San Miguel . . . or was it San Juan? I don't recall, but I've got it all written down in my luggage."

The police finally let them go, but said they might be called to testify before a coroner's jury. Charvein gave them a non-existent address in the ghost town of Lodestar.

The next afternoon, Charvein, Sandoval and Lucy were in the shop of a Los Angeles goldsmith. The cross was laid on a large piece of black cloth, allowing all the shavings and small crumbs of gold to show up. The jeweler was working on creating a more artistic cross from the crude one before him on the workbench.

It required several hours, but what finally emerged from the rough casting was a slender, fluted object fit to adorn any Christian church.

"It looks like a crusader's cross or a Templar cross," Lucy said, "It's beautiful."

Charvein knew it now appealed to her love of medieval history. She'd be content to let it go. Their alibi to the police had given them the idea of what to do with the remainder of Ezra Pitney's stolen gold.

All the shavings and small pieces of gold that were cut and filed away by the artist had been collected and now rested in a doeskin poke Lucy carried. The finished cross, they all agreed, would actually be donated to a mission church, to do with as they wished. It could never be traced to Ezra Pitney.

"This much gold will carry me for a few months, if I'm careful," Lucy hefted the small poke with the shavings. "I'm glad to be rid of that cross."

"Christ's holy cross was the object of much bloodshed," Sandoval remarked, "but it was ugly. This one is beautiful, but has been stained with the blood of greedy men."

"Well," Charvein tugged at the makeshift bandage on his swollen forearm to loosen it a little, "each of you has just enough of the original gold to get by for a time. So I guess I'll be going back to my job as a stage driver for now. Not sure how long I want to stay with that. Stagecoaches are on the way out, except in short runs. The future's in railroads, and I'm considering applying to Wells Fargo. For now, I need a job to earn some ready cash. I've spent all the $240 Pitney paid me for finding his gold in Lodestar."

"Even though he never saw any of it," Lucy grinned. "Since I found out about those Harvey Girls at the station eating place in Yuma, I think I might apply for a job with the Harvey House restaurants. I'm pretty sure there's one in this area."

"And I will go back to the desert and prospect for a time," Sandoval said, "But I'll be sure to stay clear of any more bounty hunters." He flung the end of his poncho over one shoulder and held out his arms to a cooling ocean breeze. "To avoid that damned Breem, I might even stay and prospect the deserts of California." He seemed very comfortable in his newly purchased clothes—canvas pants, rawhide moccasins and a white cotton shirt that laced up at the throat.

Charvein picked up the leather bag and flung it over his shoulder. "This thing's a good bit lighter than it was before," he commented. "I think I can carry it a ways."

"You won't have to carry it far," Lucy said. "Let's hire a buggy and deliver that cross to San Miguel, or Santa Inez . . . or was it Santa Barbara, San Juan Capistrano, or . . . ?"

ABOUT THE AUTHOR

John Michael Champlin (writing under his Confirmation name of Tim) was born in Fargo, North Dakota, the son of a large-animal veterinarian and a school teacher. He grew up in Nebraska, Missouri and Arizona before moving to Tennessee following graduation from St. Mary's High School in Phoenix.

In 1964 he declined a job offer from the U.S. Border Patrol in order to finish work on his master's degree in English, which he received from Peabody College in Nashville. Tim is the author of thirty-two historical novels, twenty-two short stories and twenty nonfiction articles.

He retired in 1994 after thirty years of work in the U.S. Civil Service.

He and his wife, Ellen, have three children and ten grandchildren.